GOOD OLE WEDNESDAY

I hear people talk. "The days go by so fast," they say. "I never have enough time." Anyone who feels that way is automatically entitled to help themselves to my last few days. And they can always have big pieces of my Wednesdays.

We have art in our homeroom on—you guessed it—Wednesdays. So what did I do? I tripped on the strap of someone's backpack, which was sticking in the aisle, and fell against the back of Odell Blake.

I became famous the very instant it happened.

"Hey, Angie, fallin' for Odell these days, huh?"

"Oh, Angie, couldn't get to him without tacklin' him, huh?"

Of course, lots of the kids were helpful. But the numbskulls were carrying the day as usual!

Dear Angie, your family's getting a divorce

CAROL NELSON

Chariot Books

ACKNOWLEDGMENTS:
Special thanks to: Paula for typing; the Saturday morning group
for prayer; to Audrey, Pat, Leonard, Jan, Linda, Patty for
checking the manuscript; to Don and Karen, Dick and Jean, Jon
and Clarice; to my parents; to all the friends who encouraged
me; and to Roy Hicks, Jr., a Shepherd's shepherd.

DEAR ANGIE
© 1980 David C. Cook Publishing Co.

Published by David C. Cook Publishing Co., Elgin, IL 60120

Printed in the United States of America
ISBN: 0-89191-246-0
LC: 79-57210

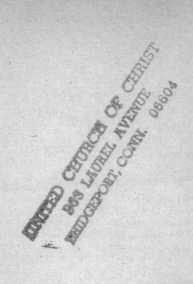

Dedicated to my family—and yours.

Contents

1
HERSHEY-BERSHEY

When I tell you all the things that have happened to me during the past three months, you will probably say, "Oh great, just what I always wanted to do: read a story about a loony!"

It's true that I did have that counselor and I did spend three days at the K. T. Center. But that was mom's idea, and she didn't know what it was like. She was just taken with the carved letters over the archway that said, People Are Our Greatest Resource.

It seems like people always want to know about a place like the center if they know you have been there, so I'll tell you. It is not a funny farm, like you always hear said.

It is A-No. 1 boring, for one thing. I was almost

the only person there who wasn't about thirty-five years old or something. I don't hate people who are thirty-five, but some of them don't do much.

Two other kids were there, for a fact, but I didn't really get to know them. Tiffany would not say anything to anyone except, "Don't touch my things." I wasn't touching them for that matter. No one was. I told her I wouldn't touch them. But then in a few minutes, she'd say again, "Don't touch my things," just as though we hadn't talked about it.

Then there was a boy about nineteen. You wouldn't believe some of the things he said, like "You may allege the past, but only the present and the future can be verified."

Even though I am not dumb and have written some poetry and other things, all my ideas sounded a little shabby alongside his. I couldn't think of a single thing to say to him. He might be a genius, for all I know.

However, a good joke I thought of was, "It's not too smart to be a genius if you end up at the Know Thyself Center."

Then there was one woman who smoked cigarettes every minute, and she would let the cigarettes burn right to the end. Right up between her fingers. That tells you right there that "knowing thyself" was not working for her.

The center was quite a bit like a hospital in some ways. At least, in the pill-taking way. But not in the arm-broken way. There were lots of people there, but they didn't do much. They told me they felt kind of blah because of the pills they were taking to make them feel calmer. One man thought the pills were poisoning him.

For a fact, I never took mine. I have a thing about pills and medicine and even cough syrup. I just think to myself, *If I were in the jungles of New Guinea, I'd have to get well without these pills, so I might as well do it here.*

Dr. Hiram Hirschmann ran the center. He talked to people twice a day: once alone and once in a group. Either way, it wasn't the world's greatest.

One of the better things he said was, "The jewels and gems every man is seeking are already locked in the vault of his own personality."

But Dr. Hirschmann had a way of saying things that more or less wrecked them. Even the one about the jewels. The way Dr. Hirschmann (some people called him Hershey-Bershey when he wasn't there) said it, it sounded kind of tired and flat.

It did start me thinking though. If my gems and jewels were locked in my vault, then Dr. Hirschmann was a holdup man, telling me to open my vault and give them to him. There was something about it that didn't follow through. Didn't "ring true" as my father sometimes says.

By lunchtime of the third day, I told Dr. Hirschmann that I wanted to go home. That's all I would say. He said they would like to keep me a bit longer. I said no. It sounds simple now, but it was creepy.

Dr. Hirschmann said he'd talk to my mom—like a postponement of what I was saying.

So I said, "Let's both talk to her now."

I may not know myself, but I knew mom. She is smart, but she is not very tough and can be easily influenced.

For instance, one time the garbage man refused to pick up the garbage. He said he wanted mom to put it in plastic bags instead of paper sacks, and he just happened to be selling the kind of bags he wanted her to use and the little ties that went with them. There was my mom standing there saying, "Well, do you think it would be all right if I just get some ties and put them around the paper sacks? I always use double sacks so they won't break."

But the garbage man said it had to be plastic sacks. I could see that mom might want to do it that way if we wished to have the best of all possible garbage. But I knew we didn't have to use plastic sacks. There was this guy holding the plastic ones up to mom and sort of bullying her.

Finally I said, "Mom, remember dad said he was going to start taking everything to the dump himself."

The garbage man had looked annoyed and suspicious. "And carry a smelly garbage can in his car all day?"

But mom was off the hook. "I guess I better check it out with my husband," she had said, and the garbage man had stalked off.

So when I heard my mom's voice on the phone that day, I started to cry. It wasn't for myself, though—not entirely. I just pictured where she would be standing and how she twists the phone cord in her fingers, and I remembered that she didn't have anyone around to say, "Oh, mom, for crying out loud!" or "Don't worry about it, mom," or "I love you."

I was crying but not bad, because I didn't want Dr. Hirschmann to talk to her. So I said, "Mom, would you please come and get me right now? I will be ready to go in twenty minutes, and I'll meet you by the door we came in."

"Oh," she said. "Well, I can try. It might take me a little longer because of the traffic."

Dr. Hirschmann was not happy with that arrangement. He signaled me that he would like to talk.

"Mom, be sure and come right away, because I think the doctor would like to give you some instructions and stuff before he leaves for the day."

"OK," she said and that was all.

Dr. Hirschmann took the phone then and said, "Mrs. Ahearne . . ." But she had hung up.

I just said, "I thought you probably wanted to talk to her in person," and went to get my things.

It might sound like I am someone who always knows how to get what I want. But I am far from it about a lot of things. This was a special case.

Dr. Hirschmann made a beeline for my mom when she got there, and so did I.

"We really feel it would be in Angie's best interests, as well as yours, to sign her in here for the customary thirty-day period," he said.

"No, mom. I'm not staying."

Dr. Hirschmann smiled at me from afar. "There is always, and especially with a gifted child like Angie, a customary period of internal and external adjustment. We often find that after the first seventy-two hours . . ."

"Mom, I think you parked in a tow-away zone. Isn't that a policeman by the car?"

"There is ample parking on the west side of the building," Dr. Hirschmann began.

"Oh, mom, it looks like Shelley is trying to climb out. Maybe that's not a policeman after all," I said. "It might be someone trying to bother her."

Things like that make my mom extremely nervous. She sort of backed up. "Perhaps I can call you, Dr. Hirschmann. I appreciate what you have done for Angie already. She hasn't been away from home much before, and it's quite a strain on all of us."

"The strain will only be increased . . ." Dr. Hirschmann began again. But I had mom's arm and we were slowly moving back. I knew I had to get out of that center. A lot had gone wrong, and I knew I had to get some help, but this was not the place.

So mom and I took ourselves, two little pieces of the center's greatest resources, and went out past the elevators, through the heavy glass doors, and across the sidewalk to the Plymouth. Right on cue, Shelley was howling miserably at the window. For once, it didn't bother me a bit.

2

AN UNFORGETTABLE SATURDAY

There is no way to tell you how things were before the center without telling you flat out that my family is not all that perfect. If you have ever seen movies of certain families where everybody has terrific solutions to everything—well, that is not my family.

Solutions are something we can definitely work on, even today. It used to be even worse.

Our big problem was not getting along. This was definitely a thing that we all didn't do. But sometimes when my parents argued, it was just about the limit to me.

Maybe my parents thought it was just as bad when Jason and Shelley and me (or I) were not getting along. There was a difference though. When we kids were not getting along, my dad could say, "Cool it! Right now."

But when my parents were not getting along, there wasn't anyone to say "Cool it." Besides they had different kinds of fights from me and Jason. I'll give you an example.

One morning when I wanted to have Cristella over to spend the night, I went looking for mom and finally found her sitting on the end of her bed.

"Not tonight, Angie," she said. She was kind of crumpled up on the end of the bed, with one knee under her chin and her other leg stretched out, making a pattern in the shag rug with her toes.

"Why not?" I asked. "I cleaned up the hallway and emptied the garbage. Without being asked." Both my folks are big on that.

"I know, babe, but it won't work tonight. Daddy and I are not getting along too well right now." Whenever I used to hear that, I would almost hit bottom.

See the difference? My dad was at work already. He wasn't even there. If Jason and I were not getting along, it would be over once he left the house. I would never have sat quietly tucked away somewhere holding off all the fun.

But my parents were different. My mom might say, "We're not getting along too well *right now*," but what she really meant was that they wouldn't be getting along later, either.

Another thing. When Jason and I fought, it was us and that was it. But when mom and dad "argued," nobody got to have any fun.

For instance, I said to her, "Oh, that's all right. I

can keep Cristella up in my room, and I can tell her you're sick or something."

"Angie," my mom said, "I said, 'No.' "

"Well, Cristella's folks probably don't get along either. Who knows?" Her parents do get along, though. But this was back when I sometimes tried to smooth things over.

I said, "Well, why don't you just get along? Why don't you say you're sorry and just forget it?"

Mom smiled a very sad smile. "It doesn't quite work that way, pet. It probably should, but it doesn't."

"Why not?" I asked. I was still holding out hope for me and Cristella, but I was also interested in what mom would say. Sometimes she shared things with me. Mostly she just tried to pull herself together when I asked her anything personal.

"Well," she said. She wasn't looking at me but still watching her foot moving on the rug. "In order to make your dad hear me, I'd probably have to tell him I thought he was right."

Now that sounded easy to me. I mean I sure wouldn't want the job of telling my dad he was wrong. So I said, "So tell him, why don't you?"

"Well, I don't think he is right. It wouldn't be honest to say I did."

Usually I would drop the subject when mom said something like that and go outside. But this time I wanted Cristella over so I stayed.

"Maybe he's a little bit right and you could just say that."

Then my mom looked sadder than ever. "Angie,

your dad doesn't care what I say, if you want to know the truth."

"Sure he does," I said. (We have gone to Steak-A-Bob tons of times when I wanted to go to King Kong's—just because my mom said she'd rather.) "Anyway," I said, "maybe he could go to a movie or something, and Cristella and you and I could pop some popcorn and play Monop—"

Suddenly mom was really mad. "Cristella. Cristella. She's all you're really thinking about, isn't she? All this talk is just another plan to get your own way. Cristella's not staying tonight. That's final."

"I hear you," I muttered and I started down the stairs. "It's just not fair; that's what I say."

By fair, I meant that when kids are not getting along, everyone just assumes that it's their own fault.

But if you are my parents and you are not getting along, then it seems like people say it's really no one's fault. It is just the way things are. If I had to list my ten worst expressions, that would be No. 1. It's just like saying, "Lay down and die."

So that was my mom's and my talk. I can't say I noticed it at the time, but looking back, I know that from that day on things never got settled again. That day was it, I guess.

I remember going over to Cristella's that morning. My mom never telephoned over there or anything. Finally, it just seemed like time to go home, so I did. Mom was sitting at the sewing machine, but she wasn't sewing. She was looking out the window, and every so often she would pass her hand across her head.

I have learned not to ask about that. You might think I should say, "Do you have a headache, mom?" but I shouldn't. She always says, "No. I'm fine," and she finds me something to do; and she begins working, too. Sometimes I might bring her an aspirin and water without saying anything. It's just the way we are.

I guess there is one thing you should know so it doesn't get too confusing later. That is about the Lord. Someone reading this might be saying to themselves, "Well, if Angie's family had just known the Lord, or trusted the Lord, then every-thing would have been fine."

But my parents trusted the Lord like you wouldn't believe. He was right up near the top of everything we did.

We went to church, read the Bible at home, said prayers at bedtime—and at mealtimes—even when my folks were mad. I can remember my mom praying sometimes at night that the Lord would protect us children from anything harmful, and to please help things be better and happier with all of us.

As you know, the Lord is very big on getting along. Mom says that he came so that we might have love and peace and joy. It seemed like a Class A reason for coming to me.

I knew the Lord, and we did a lot of things with other people who knew him, too. But quite a bit of the time, I guess I kind of forgot about him. Like you might forget about your favorite uncle when you're playing and you don't see him. You still love him and he's still your favorite uncle, but he doesn't matter to your everyday schedule. That is definitely how it was with the Lord and me at the time.

But my parents were different. They thought about the Lord about a dozen times a day at least. They liked to do things for him; they loved to hear music about him; and they hung things around the house that had parts of the Bible on them.

They weren't phony either. I know what a hypocrite is, and I tell you flat out my folks weren't like that. But I guess I've learned that adults can really blow it, too, even when they're trying to do things right. We're just lucky the Lord forgives us.

Even during this time I knew the Lord wouldn't abandon us, even if we all blew ourselves to kingdom come. That is just an expression. We're not quite that bad, I guess.

Anyway. About two weeks after our talk, when Jason and Shelley were already in bed for the night, my mom and dad asked me to sit down at the table with them. Usually that means I am not going to get to do something I had thought I would be doing. We also sit like that to look at my report card. So since I was prepared for something like that it took me quite a while to figure out what they were really saying.

Finally my mom had to just blurt it out. "Your dad is moving out, Angie. He's leaving."

"What do you mean? Moving? Will I be changing

schools?'' My ears refused to hear what they were being told.

"Your dad is moving, but we're staying here, Angie.'' My mom's voice was flat and exhausted.

"For a while, Angie. While we work some things out,'' my dad said.

My heart began pounding; then I felt myself choking. I could not say one word.

Every single thing about that talk is burned into me for life. There was a little fluted dish left on the table from dinner, and it had one radish and two slices of dill pickles on it.

My mom had on her green pantsuit, and my dad was playing with a pencil. He kept standing the pencil up, and then letting it fall down, real slow—first one end and then the other. My mom's eyes were full of tears when she looked at me. Dad didn't look at me.

Finally my dad put his hand on my shoulder and took it off. Then he put it on my head, and took it off. "We'll be seeing a lot of each other, Angie,'' he said and put his hand down around the back of my chair. After a minute he put it back in his pocket.

My mom never looked so bad. She didn't even try to stop crying like she usually does. She just sat there. She looked white and sick and cold and old, and I kept seeing this picture of her getting into bed and me pulling up the covers and tucking them under her chin the way she sometimes does when I am sick.

It's important for you to know I was thinking that because when I finally said something, I blurted out, "I'm going, too. May I?"

Believe me, I was never going to say that. It just came out.

My mom gave a shriek—even now it makes me sick at my stomach. She got up from the table, and she walked into the kitchen garbage can, which someone had moved for some reason. The garbage fell over, and my mom kind of fell over; then she got up and kept walking. I yelled, "Mom!" but she didn't look back.

My dad just sat there. I wanted to follow her, but I was afraid my dad would leave if I left the room. I stood there, and I kept hearing little noises from behind the bathroom door. Little animal noises almost.

My mind has gone over that moment quite a lot. Each time I want it to show that I didn't say that. But when the movie plays it out for me, I have said it again.

All I can say is that even though I have told you our weak point, we had some very good times, too. I don't mean just Disneyland and big things, but just times around the house.

My dad can be really weird. Like standing over me, not saying anything, but untying my shoestrings as fast as I get them tied. About ten times until we are both laughing our heads off about nothing, tying and untying faster and faster.

Or he will agree with my mom that I ought to come in and dry dishes. Then he'll grab my hands and hold me back. "Go help your mother," he'll say so mom can hear him. "You heard me."

My mom will hear what he is saying, but she can't see what he is doing. So she'll be calling, "Angie, come on, honey," and I will be trying to say, "I can't, mom. Honest." Finally my dad will say, "Angie, why are you putting your coat on? You're not going to the store now, are you?" Half the time my mom will come to see if I am, and then we will all burst out laughing.

Those are times to be proud of, as far as getting along goes. I guess you forget about those times when you are not getting along. Because my dad simply gave me a hug and turned and went into mom's and dad's bedroom.

When he came out, he was carrying a suitcase. He gave me a kiss and said good-bye.

I kept saying "Daddy wait. Please wait." But he just gave me a big squeeze.

Then he turned and left. It was a Saturday night I will never forget.

3
CRISTELLA

Mom says that we all have people who are near to our hearts. Someday, for me, that will be my husband and all of our children because that's how it works. But for now, that person is Cristella Mendez.

Since Cristella is near to my heart and her family is near to her heart, her family is also near to me. Like in math. If A is near to B and C is near to B, then A is near to C.

I want to tell you about Cristella and her family. They are part Mexican, and they have Mr. and Mrs. Mendez, Cristella, Miguel, and Ramon. They live and talk just like anybody's family. Well, they do and they don't. I love to go over there, but explaining it may be a different thing.

For instance, I can't even explain it to my mom,

and she knows Cristella and Ramon herself.

"I don't see what the Mendezes have over there that is so interesting," she says when I want to go over there.

"Nothing. I just like them," I tell her. "I like to watch them live. They're neat."

They have this kitchen chair, painted gray and red, with a fiesta decal on the back. There's a lady dancing around a big hat, a man playing the guitar, and a dog barking. I like to sit backwards in that chair, prop my arms against the back, and watch Mrs. Mendez cook.

If she had a restaurant in Washington, D.C., I bet the president of the United States would eat there. I mean it. Mom thinks I exaggerate things like that, but just because I know a person doesn't mean they're *not* the best cook either.

Cristella and Ramon are usually in the kitchen, too, doing something. Like that day my mom wouldn't let Cristella stay overnight, for instance. I went over there and Cristella was playing with Ramon. She is almost two years older than I am (it sure doesn't seem like it to either one of us, though), and Ramon is five, a year younger than Jason. But even though they are brother and sister, they could spend a whole day just kicking around together.

Ramon was driving his bulldozer on the kitchen table and shoving all the grapefruit peelings and the sugar bowl way over to the edge. Cristella just walked by and swooped it all up and plunked down a roll for him.

25

He started to bulldoze the roll to the edge of the table. Cristella began to walk her fingers up one of his arms.

"That goes up this dirt road," she said. "Up to this tunnel." She stuck the roll between his teeth and started gently pulling his hair back and up, like she was going to make a ponytail. Then she would twist it a little, let it all drop back down, and do it over again.

Ramon just sat and ate. He enjoyed everything.

There's something you should know about Ramon. He can't walk. That's why he is in the kitchen so much.

His heart was on the wrong side of his body when he was born. The Mendezes have kept the number of the fire department (it seemed funny to me that it would be the fire department) right by their phone. In the night Ramon might have an attack, which makes his breathing hard for him. Then the fire department could put him on a machine that would do part of his breathing for him.

He usually does really well during the day. In fact, Cris and I have taken him out in the wagon lots of times. He is fine except he is small for his age and his legs are real spindly. But they are all there and everything—just not strong.

Cris has taken him on her bike a lot, too. Sometimes she would let him "ride" his trike, which meant she went behind him the whole way and pushed the trike as his feet kinda "rode" on the pedals.

Anyway, right after my folks told me about dad moving, I wanted to see Cristella. But when I went over there the next afternoon, Mrs. Mendez said that Cris had taken Ramon to the store on his tricycle.

We live outside the city in a little district that has refused to be incorporated (made part of the city). Lots of times we walk to Everybody's. That's the name of the store by the gas station that sells just about everything.

I knew exactly the route Cris and Ramon would take, so I started after them. Soon I could see them up ahead, playing one of their games. Cris was driving the trike crazy, zigging and zagging, fast and slow, and sometimes making a little circle. I came up behind them without saying anything.

Ramon spotted me though. "Cris, look!" he said, pointing to me.

Cris whirled. I couldn't believe how fast! She seemed ready. Ready for anything. I had never seen her like that before. Almost fierce. Then she broke out in a big smile.

"Angie!"

It felt good to move up with them. Ramon seemed glad to see me, too. "I can whittle," he announced.

"He's gonna make a horse," Cris said. "What are you doing? You bring some money?"

"No. I was just catching up to you."

"That's OK. We got some." Cris smiled and looked at me. "What's been happening to you? You look kinda funny today."

27

"I need to ask you something. . . . What do you think a trial separation means, Cris?"

"A what?"

"A trial separation," I repeated. "My parents are having one."

Cristella was quiet. Then she stopped pushing the trike for a minute and tucked her blouse in. "I'm not sure," she said gently. "But I could try to find out if you want."

"OK. But don't tell anybody."

Suddenly Ramon turned around. "Crissy, can I get a Snickers bar?"

"You might," Cris agreed, giving his tricycle another push.

Ramon started making little war whoops and gun noises. Cristella turned back to me. "When does it start?" she said.

"It started yesterday. My dad moved out," I said. It seemed so unreal at that moment—with just Cris and Ramon and me walking to the store.

4
BLACK WEDNESDAY

You may not agree, but here's what I think: You can tell a lot about how a day is going to be by the way it feels when you first wake up.

Ever since the trial separation announcement, I had only second-rate days. Days when I would wake up and sniff the air and say to myself: "No way." Saying it doesn't always help, though. You still have to live through them.

I hear people talk. "The days go by so fast," they say. "I never have enough time." Anyone who feels that way is automatically entitled to help themselves to my last few days. And they can always have big pieces of my Wednesdays, almost any of them.

When I wake up, my first thought is, *Is it Thurs-*

day yet? Cris doesn't work in the library on Thursday, so we always eat together on that day. One particular morning I knew right away it wasn't. It was Wednesday. PE day and a no-Cristella-at-all day. I don't even get to see her between classes. Wednesday is never good, but this one!

I was looking under the bed for my sandal and finally saw that my dog, Naples, had chewed the strap that holds it on my heel almost in two. Then I heard Jason yell, "That's mine, you dumb dummy!" Next a scuffle and Shelley screaming.

Good ole Wednesday, I thought. *Don't miss a beat, do you?*

Anyway, I didn't want to go to school at all. But of course I had to. So I just pretended it was like any other day. I ate my breakfast, grabbed my lunch box, and my clarinet, and started out the door.

"Bye," I said and took off.

We have art in our homeroom on—you guessed it—Wednesdays. So what did I do that morning? I tripped on the strap of someone's backpack, which was sticking in the aisle, and fell against the back of Odell Blake just as he was taking all the water jars down to be emptied.

I became famous the very instant it happened.

"Hey, Angie, fallin' for Odell these days, huh?"

"Oh, Angie, couldn't get to him without tacklin' him, huh?"

Of course, lots of the kids were helpful, but the numbskulls were carrying the day as usual.

Finally, Mrs. Rohrbaugh made a space on the board to write down names. But she did say, "I think it's so important, and especially during art times, to be extra careful where we put our feet."

One time I wrote a poem about her:

Rohrbaugh, Rohrbaugh,
Do you like to snore? Ha.
Sleeping on the floor, ma.
Cause we are so poor, pa.

It doesn't really mean anything, but I like it.

Anyway, that was Wednesday's opening shot, I guess you'd say. After art, I still have Mrs. Rohrbaugh for two more hours. And, of course, all my good buddies with their new crop of Odell jokes.

After art (remember I am telling you this day just like it happened) I had homeroom—so, library. Forty minutes in the library to take notes on our library paper. I was doing a library paper on Thoreau. So I was supposed to look up Thoreau and the romantic movement in several books and take notes. Mrs. Rohrbaugh thinks we are back in the romantic movement in this country, even today. Could be. It's not the world's greatest, that's for sure.

Anyway, I came back into the room that Wednesday with exactly no notes on Thoreau or on the romantic movement. I could tell Mrs. Rohrbaugh was annoyed with several of us, but she was trying to hold it in, I guess.

I was listening to announcements and wondering when this upside-down day would be over when someone touched my arm. I turned around to see who it was, and I saw Julie pointing to the floor. Right beside my right heel was a note. I dropped my pencil and bent over carefully to pick them both up.

Just as I was about to look at it, Mrs. Rohrbaugh said something—a name. *Angie.* It was me.

"Angie, will you please come here?"

I began to get up. My skirt was still sopping from the watercolor water.

"No," Mrs. Rohrbaugh said. "Bring that piece of paper with you, please."

By now everyone was looking. They were pretending not to, but they were.

I picked the paper up and started forward with it. I was thinking, *Anyway, it's not my note.* I hadn't written one to anybody, so whoever wrote it had to answer for it.

Mrs. Rohrbaugh said, "I see you have a note, Angie."

I said nothing.

She said, "Earlier in the hour we were supposed to be writing notes. In the library weren't we?"

"Yes, ma'am," I said.

The whole class was sitting there like a bunch of scholars with notebooks crammed with library notes. I mean, really.

"You didn't write any notes then, did you, Angie?"

Boy. Mrs. Rohrbaugh is always making points. She digs points. I'm telling you. I knew this was going to be one. "No, ma'am."

"But now you have."

"This is not my note," I said.

"Really? Whose name is on the front of it, please?"

I thought for a minute; it really might not be my note, you know—a note to me. Maybe I was supposed to pass it to Kathy or—well, I didn't really think it would be to Grace, but I guess it might. Anyway, when I looked down, I saw some writing I couldn't quite recognize, though it seemed like I ought to be able to. It said Anjie—not Angie.

"Well?" Mrs. Rohrbaugh was waiting for an answer.

I heard the class getting restless, and I could see Jim and David starting to make remarks already.

Somehow I said, "Angie." It was awful. I had horrible, wild feelings choking up in me. But my voice was real quiet.

"Pardon me?" Mrs. Rohrbaugh said.

I cleared my throat. "It says 'Angie' on the note," I said meekly, looking at a spot on the blackboard just behind Mrs. Rohrbaugh's head.

"Read it," she said. "Turn around and face the class and read it to them so everyone can hear."

That was when this thing happened. It was like I wasn't even there. I was somewhere nearby watching Mrs. Rohrbaugh and the girl with this note. This girl, for some reason, didn't care at all about the note. She simply opened it and turned to face the class.

She was not embarrassed and did not care what the note said. Just to show how little she cared, she began to read it as soon as she spotted the first word and read it to the class as she read it to herself.

"Dear Anjie: LuAnn said your family is getting a divorce because your dad goes around town with his girl friend. If you eat with me, I'll give you my grapes.

Melanie."

This girl looked at the note for a minute. Then my heart started to pound in my chest, in my ears, and even down my arms. My hands began to shake, and my hands had a note in them. And the girl was gone. There was only me. I wanted to lie down, but I couldn't. So I ran.

The classroom door, which usually sticks, started to stick; then it flew right open. My feet were doing everything without me.

As I ran, I heard Mrs. Rohrbaugh calling my name. Then I thought maybe it wasn't my name. Maybe it was *Anjie*, not *Angie*, she was calling. I heard a car honk just as I reached the far curb. I kept thinking over and over. Mother. Be there.

In my mind, I saw mom making cookies. I was running, and a girl twisted her ankle. It was me. Sorry, foot. *That's just the way things are*, I thought. The girl's face was wet. The watercolors hadn't splashed up that high. Cristella. Where are you? Mother, be home. I remember telling Jesus I would never do anything wrong again if he would make her be home. I promised.

The house was empty. The breakfast dishes were not picked up. Merced's kittens crowded around me, hoping that I would play with them.

There was something trying to get into my mind. I didn't want it there, but there was a girl who would. Anjie.

A car crunched in the driveway. Then the thought sneaked in, just when I thought I was safe. It was a car I had seen one day.

I had looked up from the soccer field and seen a car moving away from a stop sign. I had yelled, "Dad!" Then I had run a ways down the field just for fun. "Dad!" Then I had felt stupid. It wasn't dad at all. It was some man and his wife, and I hadn't seen the wife at first because she was so close to her husband.

It had looked like my dad's car. I didn't want to think about that now. But it was too late, see. All the circuits were connected and the answer flashed in the girl's mind. I saw it by mistake.

That was my dad. How could it be? It was dad. Taking a little girl home who got sick or something. Why wasn't I told?

"If you will eat with me today, you can have my grapes." Eat your own stupid grapes, Melanie Snotnose. My dad was taking a little girl home from school because she had a headache. No, that was mom who gets headaches. Wait. Was it mom? No, mom would have said.

I saw the car again. There were two heads close together. One was the sick girl. No, it was a grown-up head. One was my dad. One was . . . was . . . was not.

The garage door opened and shut.

"Angie," came my mom's voice. "Angie, is that you in there?" My mom appeared in the door. "What are you doing home now, honey? Are you sick or something?"

The note was for Anjie. I am Angie.

"No," I said. "I'm not. Melanie's sick. But everyone thought it was me."

Mom came over by me. I couldn't seem to let her know.

"Honey, you're all hot and sweaty."

"No. Oh, mom, I don't know. Everything is mixing up, and I can't straighten things out, because Melanie tells it wrong and now they think it's me."

Mom put her arms around me and pulled me down next to her on the couch. She held me like I was still lap-size. "Jesus," she said. "Jesus. It's Angie and me. We're so lost, Jesus. So lost. Please, can you help us?"

I wanted to tell my mom that this didn't have anything to do with Jesus. But I felt such a peace sitting there with her, and tiredness—the good kind of tiredness—settled over me.

So I didn't say anything. The girl was gone. Only mom and I were there with the kittens. I guess I fell asleep.

5
ANJIE

When I went back to school the following Monday, it was as if I had lived a lifetime since I had last been there. But I really hadn't done much at all.

I spent Thursday and Friday cleaning out closets and cupboards and putting down new shelf paper in the kitchen. Saturday, I spent the whole day in my room trying to fix it up the way I wanted it. Sometimes I listened to the radio, but mostly I just moved furniture around, hung pictures, and washed and ironed curtains.

This was odd because no one told me to do these things, and I had never done any of them before. When I got all the way through, I honestly couldn't remember what my room had looked like when I started. I thought I would take Shelley out for an ice cream cone when I finished, but then she sat right in the middle of my bed and wet it without batting an eye, so I didn't.

The only thing I noticed that was really strange was that I didn't want to see Cristella. And I didn't want to go back to school. As long as I was home, doing little jobs, I was fine. But when I thought of leaving the house and going back to school . . .

Anybody who could make Odell jokes from a person tripping over a backpack could have a field day with a girl who announces to the world that her family's falling apart and then runs for her life.

Never in my life did I want to see Mrs. Rohrbaugh again. Nor anyone in my school. I wanted to live all by myself. Or go to school and do the work if I didn't have to talk to anybody. I could be like Grace—just come and go and eat alone until I graduated.

I got along fine, thinking of this prospect, until Sunday afternoon. Then I knew Monday morning was coming up no matter what I wanted. I knew, too, that I would have to go.

My mom was in no condition to have me pull some goody on her like I had on Wednesday. She was almost around the bend without that.

She went around the house with a wool sweater pulled down over her blouse and the furnace turned up to eighty-five degrees. Even so, she'd wrap her arms around herself like cold people do and just sort of wander from room to room. She sat in the kitchen all day Friday and watched me put in shelf paper. She didn't offer to help or offer any suggestions. She just watched. I was doing it because we had done it in home ec earlier in the year, and I thought it was neat. My mom sat perched on the edge of a chair and watched me as if she were Shelley or someone.

The days went on forever without dad coming home at night. Our meals were weird. My mom never thought about fixing anything unless someone told her to. She wasn't hungry and she forgot. She would pick up something in the living room that belonged in the bathroom, like a hairbrush or something, and she would wander around with it—and finally put it down in the dining room.

Then she would read the newspaper. When she had read for a while, she would lay her head down right in the middle of the paper and close her eyes. She would stay there until someone asked her for something.

On Saturday, when she saw me fixing my room, she suggested a real great plan: How I could do my room with a new canopy for my bed and new curtains and a rug to climb out of bed onto. She even talked about two little pictures of ballerinas she had seen at The Grotto, and where we could hang them. Then she put a pillow down on the floor and fell fast asleep. I finally remembered to put a blanket over her. When she woke up, she never mentioned any of the things we had talked about for my room.

Jason and Shelley were hideous. I had decided by Saturday morning that if Jason or Shelley told me one more time that I was not the mother and they didn't have to do what I said, I would step aside and let them do what they had always wanted to do: murder each other. No lie. Jason was slamming doors, taking crackers into his room, jumping on his bed, and spilling stuff everywhere. He even decided to paint his basketball backstop—without asking. He slopped paint all over the patio and the lawn. When he went back for the ladder, he decided—without asking—to take a bike ride down to Everybody's instead, so he left the paint sitting there to get mucky.

Shelley decided to take her dolls swimming, even the ones that aren't supposed to get wet. She threw them all in the bathtub and turned the water on full blast, ruined everything for about fifty feet in every direction; then decided to get on her own swimsuit. She couldn't find it so she went outside with nothing on and turned on the hose. When I tried to bring her inside, she bit my arm.

I do not know how I got through those days except in a way I didn't. That thing about that girl was on my mind. I knew there was a girl who could come and be me, and she could manage a lot that I couldn't because she was cold and strong. She would not care what happened to any of us, but she could get through it. She, well, like she wanted to take over, if I would only let her. I knew about her in a way. She could say, "Good-bye, dad"; let Jason and Shelley go; and watch mom and even Angie drop off and never look back.

I didn't want this girl around. I suspected that if I couldn't do something right, she was going to do it without me. *Maybe she's Anjie*, I thought.

By Sunday afternoon, I realized that Angie could never go back to school by herself. She was going to have to have help—and it looked like it would have to be Anjie. This may not make any sense to you, but it is in fact what happened.

I hadn't forgotten about the Lord. It's just that I didn't know exactly how to get in touch with him for this particular thing. My parents knew him better than I did, it seemed like, and yet somehow he hadn't kept them from this trial separation.

Anyway, I went to school. I did not go to orchestra. I just went to school at the regular time. On Monday, you know, most people have a lot of stuff to share and plenty on their minds. But I could see that after they greeted me and were starting to talk about junk, my little performance was coming right back in their minds again.

I just put away my books and started writing down assignments from the left side of the board. I might have done something better than that, but I couldn't think what it was. I wanted to tuck myself in and be left alone.

When lunch came, several of the girls asked me to eat with them. I was going to at first, but then I felt funny. I felt like they had probably cooked it up together. Like the poster for the Foster Parents Program: Take a kid to lunch. You'll be glad you did.

I'm not trying to make excuses. I started to go; then I didn't. I said I was going to make up some work during my lunch hour. As I watched them leave, I felt that tomorrow would be easier.

And it was. They asked me and waited on Tuesday. By Wednesday they asked, but you could tell they expected to hear, "No," and on Thursday everybody knew I had lunch with Cristella.

I hadn't gotten thickheaded enough to refuse lunch with Cristella. I sat where I always waited for her, and then I saw her coming. She is so beautiful, I think. She has dark hair and her eyelashes match, and then she often wears white or red or yellow up by her face. She could win a prize any day even if she didn't know there was going to be a contest and she hadn't done anything special. Many people don't seem to notice how pretty she is, though. I could never figure that out. They thought other girls were just as pretty or prettier who were not nearly as good-looking. You just have to take my word for it, I guess.

Cristella couldn't find out anything about trial separations. I figured that, too. But I knew she'd try.

I couldn't tell her about the note. But I did say Melanie thought my parents were going to get a divorce. Cris just looked at me.

"They aren't though, Cris. I know my folks. They just don't believe in things like that. This trial separation is very hard on them, and I'm sure it isn't a divorce."

Just as soon as I said, "I'm sure it isn't a divorce," I knew for certain that it was. But I didn't say that to Cris. Not then.

She switched the subject, and we started to talk about the assembly we had had on Tuesday about fire prevention. She wanted to know where I had been sitting, because she had looked for me and hadn't seen me. The fireman had shown us all kinds of equipment they keep, and Cris had wanted to show me the one they used on Ramon sometimes.

That's Cris, though. She probably heard everything that was said during the whole assembly. I had written *Fire Prevention* across the top of one page in my notebook; then I filled the rest of the page with the words *Fire Prevention* written like some movie star might write it or something. I get off on things like that all the time.

I guess I had even heard them talk a little about the machine they use on Ramon, but I didn't really connect it with him until Cris mentioned it at lunch. Cris is special. She sees things for what they really are.

I knew I might not see Cris until the following Thursday to really talk. Mom had decided to take us kids and go to my grandparents' for the weekend. I love my grandparents a lot, but I really wanted to have Cristella over to spend the night. I mentioned it to her, and she said we could stay together a week from Friday.

Finally, I came to the end of that crazy week. I didn't think a whole lot more about Anjie and Angie, but I hadn't forgotten. When Mrs. Rohrbaugh spoke to me or called on me, it was always Anjie who answered. Also if Melanie or LuAnn were nearby, I automatically went into being Anjie.

It was kind of a game at first. When you play games, they can change sometimes. It was a game, but it wasn't. I was hacking away at the old Angie who just wanted to forget the whole thing and be friends again. Anjie wanted to remember, even when it was hard. She wanted Mrs. Rohrbaugh and LuAnn and Melanie to remember, too. She even wanted to be kind of mysterious about that note and about what was happening so kids could see that she was not just anybody.

It was a game. I knew that. Sometimes, for fun, I would write my name as Anjie on assignments for Mrs. Rohrbaugh. Then I did it once or twice for other teachers. Nobody seemed to say anything about it.

At home I was always Angie. With Cristella I was always Angie. With the Lord I would always be Angie. Sometimes, though, at school I wasn't. It was a game, really. One day I noticed the strangest thing. Anjie had a different handwriting than Angie.

6

INVITATION

Cynthia Hollis and Mary Jane Knutsen are eighth graders and so is Cristella. I am a seventh grader. To Mary Jane and Cynthia, that is the same as not existing. If you did not have a pulse, you could not be less alive than if you were a seventh grader, according to Cynthia and Mary Jane.

In fact, Boyd told Cristella that Mary Jane sometimes went around with a high school boy in his car, and her mom knew it and everything.

If you want to know what I thought about this, I couldn't even think about it without shuddering. Why would anybody want to get in a car with a high school boy? I knew I wouldn't be able to think of one thing to say.

I like boys a lot, though. There is one in my math class I like to sit next to. We sometimes say to each other: "What'd you get for number five?" and "Looks like old Eddy may be taking this class over again at the rate he's going."

Once he said, "Did you watch the Vikings last night? Man, oh man!"

I'll even go so far as to tell you that I wrote his name sometimes in my fire-prevention handwriting, but I'd rather not say what his name is. For one thing his name is not as neat as he is.

I could see myself getting into a car with him to go on a field trip or something. Otherwise, no. But anyway, he is in seventh grade—not in high school.

I will say this about Mary Jane Knutsen. She is "up" compared to what I am. She is a girl you could see in a car with a high school boy right off.

She and Cynthia are always together, and there is always a crowd of other girls around them at lunch hour and between classes. They don't care who's around them. Even seventh-grade girls can stand there, but they don't talk to them.

One time when I was with them, Mary Jane was sitting next to Cynthia and she was just fingering the charms on her bracelet. When she would come to a certain one, she and Cynthia would just die laughing, and then they would say things. Like Mary Jane would say, "You know about this one, don't you?" and Cynthia would say, "That was that Friday night, wasn't it?" and they would both laugh.

Then Mary Jane would flick her hair off the collar of her blouse with her fingernails. She has fingernails like you wouldn't believe. The only thing they might be like are Fush-She-Ko's in *The Diary of the Orient*. I'll tell you one thing. When I first saw those fingernails, I knew I wasn't quite a person compared to her, let alone a girl.

Cynthia Hollis is not quite as marvelous as Mary Jane, but she hangs in there pretty good. She also has a charm bracelet and fingernails and the whole works. Cynthia is skinnier and her clothes kind of hang on her in various places; but her clothes are always muchy-much, sometimes even more than Mary Jane's.

Cynthia and Mary Jane both wear these stilty shoes that my mom won't even pause over in the shoe store. I know there is something about them that I like, but I also know they wouldn't work on me.

Anyway, anybody is going to see right off that I am not as far down the road of life as Mary Jane Knutsen. Or Cynthia either, although that's not so much an issue.

But at school I wasn't just good old Angie anymore either. There was a lot of Anjie. I still didn't eat with anyone except on Thursdays. In fact, I took a notebook and just mostly wrote in movie-star handwriting or tried a few poems. My heart wasn't really in it. I thought a lot about my dad, but I didn't write anything about that.

I knew there were kids at school whose parents didn't just have a trial separation but had a regular divorce. I knew it must make them sad, but it didn't seem to completely wipe them out. That's me though. My mom says everything seems to get to me the way it does to her.

One day when I was going out of the lunchroom and I walked over to the big can to throw away my orange peels, I heard my name *Angie* called by— who says the age of miracles is over?—Mary Jane Knutsen.

I automatically hid my fingernails under my books and walked over there.

Mary Jane's hair was feathered and blown back. Mine was—well, let's not go in to that. My light brown hair is quite a bit like the rest of me. Not quite there, yet. My eyes are, you guessed it—OK to see out of and everything, but not quite fjord blue. I'm not really skinny, but I might as well be when I get near Mary Jane.

"Angie. That is your name, isn't it?" Mary Jane laughed like it was my own fault if my name was something else.

"Yeah," I said. Immediately I wished I had said *yes*.

"Are you the girl who is good friends with that Mexican girl in the other class? What's her name . . . Missy?"

Something in me gathered, like an animal on its guard, I guess. But you may as well know that it also felt good to me that Mary Jane Knutsen knew my name and had called me over. I hate myself when I'm like that, but there it is.

"Cristella. We call her Crissy sometimes. Yes. Why?"

"Cristella. Oh, Crissy." Mary Jane and Cynthia

looked at one another and giggled. Then they looked back at me. "Is Crissy your best friend, Angie?"

I will say that Mary Jane or no, all I wanted was to get out of there. I mean, here's just a simple question that anybody could answer, but some questions asked in certain ways don't have right answers.

"Yeah, I guess you could say that," I finally said.

Mary Jane giggled, and Cynthia quickly joined her. "Oh, we could say it? I think that's cute. Crissy and Angie. That's sweet—Crissy's so pretty. Does she live by you?"

"Not too far."

"Do you think that you and Crissy could come to a party at my house, Angie?"

My heart started pounding again. I would rather have done almost anything than go to a party at Mary Jane's. But here's how I am. I feel guilty that someone wants me to do something with them, and I don't return their feelings. Anyway, if I had had my choice between going to Mary Jane's for a party and having Old Man Harris's Doberman get out of his fence and chase me five breathless blocks like he did last summer, I would take the Doberman. I have a better bike this year for one thing.

Now that I told you what I was thinking, you can be as surprised as I was when I blurted out, "Sure. We'd love it. I can check with Cris, but it sounds like fun to me."

Now that is an answer that didn't come from

Angie or Anjie, either one. That is an answer that came from a big, fat chicken that has always lived in me and who comes out to lay an egg every so often.

I should probably also tell you that even though Mary Jane had high school boys in cars who liked her, she didn't do too bad in junior high, either. Everywhere she went, there were always a few boys sitting in a group not far away. If you would ever want to see something sappy, you should put them on your list. They would sit there after lunch. Then one of them would say, "Hey, Mary Jane!" and she'd look over; and then they'd pull some stunt to show off.

Anyway, they were there then. She looked across the two empty tables at them; then up at me.

"You like to have fun, Angie?" She asked it in such a slow, chocolate way, as though it were a question that could have two answers. I don't know why but it embarrassed me. The boys laughed and poked each other and began to carry on some elaborate deal under the table.

Mary Jane let her hair fall forward, and she took one little curl and wrapped and unwrapped her little finger with it.

She is just more "up" than I am. I didn't want to be like her, but I didn't hate her. She was always doing something that you didn't mind watching.

"Sure," I said. I felt like that bimbo in the Phantom of the Opera cartoon. Mary Jane didn't seem to notice though.

"Does Crissy like to have fun, too?" she asked. The boys were outdoing themselves by this time, gesturing, laughing, and throwing themselves backwards against their chairs. Cynthia ran her little finger, painted light pink, back and forth across her bottom lip. I can't tell you why, but it seemed to me like it was almost evil. Don't ask me. It just did.

I nodded, wishing I could end the conversation. But for some reason I couldn't just leave.

"Do you think you and Crissy would be able to spend the night?" Mary Jane said sweetly. The boys were at the top of their form by now. They assured everyone within listening distance that they would be able to spend the night. Anytime. Anytime at all. Poke, poke, poke. Ha, ha, ha, ha. Yeah. Yeah.

I had to say something so I could leave. I guess I'm full of excuses like my mom says. Anyway, I said, "Sure, I guess so. I think we can."

"Oh, neat!" Mary Jane said. She looked as though Cris and my coming over was the best of all possible events. "That's super!" She just sat and looked at me.

I can't tell you how I felt. My fingernails were bent double under my books. I remembered one button was off my blouse, and I had pinned it shut real puckery after P.E.

Cynthia did everything the way Mary Jane did, including look at me from head to foot. This one guy named Norman kept yelling, "Hey, Mary Jane, did you say it would be super if I come, too?" She didn't even look at him.

I started to back off.

"Don't you want to know when it is?" she said softly.

"Oh, sure. When is it?"

"This Friday." That was the night Cris and I had agreed to stay with each other. It was as if she knew that without being told.

"You know where I live?" she said.

"Somewhere on Dexter Point, isn't it?" I said. I knew her house by heart from driving by it.

"It's the white house, second from the end," she said. "Why don't you and Crissy come about seven o'clock?"

"I'll have to check with Cris," I said lamely.

"I'll check with Cris," she said. "I'll tell her you're going, and then I know she'll want to." She tossed her hair back and smiled. "See you Friday, Angie. OK?"

All I wanted to do was go home and hide. But at that point I still had speech, health, and current events to go. For anybody who still doesn't know what day this was, I'll give you a clue: It starts with a *W* and it goes on forever.

7
BAGS OF FUN?

When my mom heard that I was spending the night at Mary Jane Knutsen's, she got all dressed up and took me downtown to buy me new pajamas, a new dress, and some sandals that hadn't been chewed. Of course with Naples, it's just a question of time. My dad always says, "If Nape hasn't chewed it, depend on it. He thinks you want him to." My dad, honestly.

And my mom, too. New pajamas. Here I was trying to get a fast case of plague, and my mom was trying to make a Zulu out of me. She didn't know Mary Jane, but she knew Dexter Point and she knew my pajamas. Also, she was forever and a day asking me if there weren't "any other little girls in my class besides Cristella." She didn't mind Cristella the way you might think—like some people don't like Mexicans or whatever. She just thought I worshiped Cristella too much. How's that?

My mom can be an amazing amount of fun when she cuts loose and isn't afraid of what anybody is going to think. Especially on vacation. Once we rented this house with a swimming pool off Okay Creek in Idaho. Grandma and Grandpa Ahearne live in Idaho.

Us kids had a tug-of-war with my dad across the pool, and of course he pulled us into the pool with our suits on. He was so sure he would win that he left his pants and shoes on. While he was standing there laughing at us, mom sneaked up behind him, made a sudden run, and pushed him in.

He turned around in the water when he came up, and said, "I'm going to get you for that."

She was laughing. "No, you're not."

"I bet you fifty dollars I'm going to baptize that dress."

Mom was all dressed up because she was supposed to meet Grandma Birdie for a luncheon.

"Fifty dollars! You're on," she said, and she jumped—whacko—right in the pool with the luncheon clothes on, right down to her patent-leather shoes. My dad laughed so hard he cried, and she laughed, too.

That was a long time ago.

The Mary Jane thing was coming in on me a million miles an hour. There would be no fun at Mary Jane's, that much I knew. I sometimes think of myself as an expert on fun, because it's my favorite thing. If something is fun, I know it whether I get to do it or not. If it isn't, I can almost smell it.

There was something in the stilty shoes and the fingernails and the charm bracelets that was more than you could see, but I knew for a fact that it was not fun. It was something else. I told my mom I would rather just pop some popcorn and play pitch with her and Cristella—and Jason could even play if he wouldn't cheat. That's the thing with my mom, though. She wants me to have this fairy-tale type of good time that can only be had at a party like Mary Jane's.

Something was bothering me more, and that was Cristella. Of course I couldn't talk about that to mom, because she thought that Mary Jane had invited Cristella at my insistence, and she was upset with me about that. Can't you just picture that? Me saying, "Mary Jane, I'm afraid I must insist you invite Cristella Mendez to your party or you can forget about me coming."

It was much more likely that Cristella had been invited and had said she wouldn't go without me. No use asking her though. She'd never say.

But I wanted to know why they suddenly wanted either of us at their old stupid party. Could it be I didn't want to share Cristella? Was I afraid that if other people found out how neat she was, she wouldn't want me for a friend anymore?

I play Truth or Dare with myself sometimes. Like in this case, I said, "Is it true?" If I say it's not true when it is, then I have to do something I dare myself to do. I think of terrible dares for myself. Like daring myself not to eat chocolate for the whole month.

So I told the truth. I *was* sort of afraid Mary Jane and her buddies were going to take Cris. But for a fact, I knew there was something left over. Something worrying me that I couldn't get myself to look at yet. Something about Cristella and not me.

I mean, what did those girls want with us?

My mom ended up getting me a bunch of stuff that was worse than going the way I was before. But I didn't care. I had one thought about that party: Get it over with. Cristella looked nice, though. Naturally she hadn't gotten all gaudied up with a new dress and shoes and new pajamas and all—just everything clean and nice. By the way, I do not worship Cristella, if you're remembering about that. But I do know her good points.

Mom drove us up to Dexter Point, and we walked up the long driveway. When we rang the doorbell, there was a long wait, and finally Cynthia came to the door. She said, "Oh!" Then, "Come on in. . . . Mary Jane, those girls are here."

Now, I mean, how's that? That's not too dumb a way to put it, is it? Cynthia is one girl I felt I could have lived without knowing.

Mary Jane came out. She was wearing cute clothes but not party clothes. They were pants and a tee shirt with a shirt over. So, obviously, was Cynthia.

"Hey," Mary Jane said, looking at me with a tiny smirk. "You guys didn't have to get all dressed up.

Some of us are just going to kick around a little bit."

Cynthia laughed, and Mary Jane giggled. "Cindy, you better be good," she said, and Cynthia burst out into another wild laugh. Mary Jane turned back to us. "Crissy and Angie," she said softly. "I guess we could say they're best friends." She smiled. "Come on in."

If you are wondering why we didn't go home, you would do better than to ask me. All I know is that there was so much showy stuff going on. Mary Jane wasn't really saying anything snotty. Cynthia could just be having a good time. It wasn't right, but there was no way to prove it was all that wrong.

What if I had said, "Come on, Cristella, let's go." Mary Jane and Cynthia could have looked at me and said, "Huh? You just got here. What have we done?"

That was seven o'clock. We did nothing. Finally at about quarter to eight, two more girls arrived. They were eighth graders. But none of us were doing anything. Mary Jane put on some records, and we kind of followed her from room to room. She did her nails, with all of us watching. She talked on the phone a little bit real quietly.

The other girls (Jody and Diane) were laughing with each other about how they had worked it out so they could come.

"Our folks weren't going to let us after last time," they said. All the girls laughed, and Jody and Diane launched into a big thing about how they had told their folks this and told them that. They outdid each other telling how melodramatic and clever they had been.

Cristella was like an angel, I kid you not. She just looked quietly at the girls, and they would finally see her looking at them and kinda wilt. She was not having fun, but she was not upset. She looked at some magazines and finally found a *Teen Scene*, one that she had started reading in the library.

Me? My mind was racing like mad. I couldn't figure out why those girls would have trouble with their folks after "last time." If this time was anything like last time, there was nothing to it. Not even anybody's grandmother could mind a boring mess like this.

But the girls were not bored. They were waiting. They talked about boys, played records, rolled out their sleeping bags—but they were waiting. The party wasn't starting yet for some reason. The next hour had to be the most boring time of my life.

At nine o'clock, the girls started going to the windows and looking out. Cynthia said she thought she heard a noise in the driveway, and they all ran to the door and opened it and looked down the driveway. That's when I finally turned to Cristella.

"Bags of fun, huh?" I said.

Cristella laughed. "Want to go?"

I could not believe my ears. "Cris, are you kidding? Could we?" The idea seemed so daring and so exciting. We knew there would be anger or hurt feelings or something to consider.

"What are they looking for?" I asked Cristella.

"I don't know," she said. "Probably Mary Jane's boyfriend is supposed to stop by, and she wants to see him."

"Can you believe this, Cris? I mean, I would rather be taking care of Shelley and Jason." Suddenly, I thought of mom, and I wanted to be with her.

The girls came back inside, and, they got some food out of the refrigerator. That got me a little interested. We were deciding whether to have sundaes or caramel corn when suddenly we heard something. Plenty.

Three cars pulled up in the driveway. The doorbell began ringing and ringing until the whole living room and dining room echoed with it. All the girls were screaming. "Mary Jane, they're here, they're here! How many of them are there? Oh, no, Mary Jane, don't let them in yet. Wait a minute!"

Mary Jane and Cynthia were laughing, and Mary Jane was shushing the girls up and peeking out. Cris asked one of them, "Who are they? Who's here?"

The girl gave us both a stare like a trapped little animal. "Oh, the guys! They're right out there. M-a-a-a-a-r-r-r-r-ry Jane, help me! You've got to HELP ME!" she screamed suddenly. But she was giggling wildly and rolling her eyes at the door. "I want my mama," she said coyly.

For me, the whole thing was like a slow-motion nightmare. I was scared; there's no point calling it something else. With all the yelling and the pounding at the door and the windows, there had to be about twenty guys out there, and they sounded like high school.

Cristella was frightened, but she was not screaming. She looked at me, and a kind of shudder passed over her. "Didn't you say it was time to be going?" she said.

I agreed, and we started toward the back. The girls were all clustered around the front door, and Mary Jane was saying, "Tell them to stop pounding. They can come in if they won't mess things up. But you have to get them to promise."

There was more yelling and pounding; then one person yelling and some of the others finally stopping. I couldn't wait any longer. I grabbed Cris by the hand, and we went through the utility room and out the back door.

8
YOUR GIRL, JOHNNY

It was cool outside, but it wasn't as dark as I had wished it would be. I could see myself and Cris so plainly I knew we had to find a place to hide. There was nothing out back but a garden shed and some tennis courts. Something that looked like the edge of a swimming pool was showing from the side of the house.

I called it a shed. Actually the structure out back had a little potting shed at one end attached to a greenhouse. But the greenhouse part was separated by a little door and a walled-in walkway. There was a padlock on the door but it hadn't been locked. It was just hanging there.

I pulled Cristella in and closed the door. The only thing on the inside was a little bolt to keep the door from swinging. As soon as I saw that I wanted to go somewhere else, but it was too late. It seemed like only one minute or less before there were people at the back door.

"Crissy! Angie!" It was Mary Jane. Then, because we were so nearby, we could hear them whispering. Soon they didn't even bother to whisper.

"Well, I got her here for Johnny, but now Johnny is going to have to find her. You guys could have come a little more quietly." It was Mary Jane talking to some boy.

The boy laughed. "Hey, Johnny! Your girl is out there somewhere looking for you!" They heard answering noises inside. Then the boy said to Mary Jane, in an undertone, "What'd you say her name was?"

"Cristella," Mary Jane said. "Only be quiet. We do have some neighbors out there somewhere."

"Yeah. Hey, John, Big John! Cristella is out there looking for you, and she can't find you. Shame on you."

John lumbered through the back door, followed by three or four more guys. "What about us?" one of them said. "Isn't she looking for us?"

Mary Jane's boyfriend spoke up. "Now, don't get greedy you guys. Cristella's got a big heart." He turned and raised his voice. "Don't you, Cristella?"

I honestly thought if they didn't hear my heart pounding they had to be deaf.

Mary Jane's boyfriend went on. "Take my word

for it, Johnny, Cristella is waiting for you either in the cowshed there or in the swimming pool. Either way, you can't lose." There was lots of laughter and shouting and egging Johnny on.

Then Mary Jane said, "There's another girl there, too. Angie."

The boys behind John let out a whoop. "Hey, hey, all right. Hey, Angie. Angie, where are you? You see, I have this problem, Angie."

"Shut up, you guys," Mary Jane's boyfriend warned. "Just cool it. Somebody is going to hear us and call the cops."

Suddenly there was the noise of loud laughter and glass breaking inside. Then a scream. Mary Jane turned and started in. "Jerry, you tell your buddies to get out of here right now. My mom is going to kill me."

"Not us, Mary Jane. We're not going anywhere, man," the guys in the backyard said. "We're not doing nothin'."

Mary Jane ignored them. "Get those guys out of this house, Jerry. I mean it."

Jerry walked back in beside her. "Hey, guys! There's a whole bunch of girls hiding out in the backyard. Why don't you find them so we can get this party rolling."

There was a lot more yelling from inside and another sound of breaking glass. Four more guys piled through the back door, whooping and swearing and yelling. "Where?" "Yeah, where?" they yelled.

Cristella had sunk down in the corner, but I was

watching through the slit in the door. I couldn't stand not to.

I'll tell you this. There was not one neat guy in the whole bunch. I mean, that's what they were—all guys who were the numskull type, just like in junior high. They were dumb. They were following one another around, trying to act real with-it or something, but they were just stupid. A lot of stupid jerks who had to gang together and pump each other up, just to go to a junior high school party. There was not one guy, except maybe Mary Jane's boyfriend, who could have stood up to the guy I sit next to in math.

While they were milling around, squeaking to each other about what they would do when they found Cristella and Angie, I guess something happened to me. I got angry.

It seemed like the iron that was in Anjie suddenly shot through little quaking Angie. I was furious to be standing there waiting for some creeps to decide we were in there and push in the door.

I leaned over and picked up a long, pointed weed puller. I held it up in front of me. *If any of them try to come in here . . .* I thought. Then I got a picture of that. I saw how they could just lift the weed puller right out of my hand like it was nothing. I looked over and I saw the Indoor/Outdoor Insect Killer. It was a big tall can, and it had a skull and crossbones on it. I put the weed puller down and picked up the spray. I looked over at Cris, and she gave me a tight, little smile.

That was all—just a scared little smile. But I knew

I couldn't use that spray. I just tried to smile, too, and set it back on the shelf. I noticed though that it said to keep it away from direct heat, because the can could explode, and not to puncture it.

We waited.

Even stupid boys can finally find some kind of a leader for themselves. With these guys, they just kept urging this Johnny—big, heavy, surly looking guy—to find his girl and Angie so the "party can get rollin', man."

Everybody had to know where we were anyway, it seemed to me. There wasn't anywhere else to be. Nevertheless, Johnny went back to consult Mary Jane and Jerry. They both came out.

"Cristella! Angie!" she said. "Crissy! Angie! Come on out, you guys."

The boys were making a wonderful chorus, I'm telling you. "Here, Crissy, Crissy, Crissy."

Finally Mary Jane walked over to the shed we were in. "The door's locked from the inside," she said. "They're in here."

I will never forget that. She did not say, "Hey, are you guys in there?" or do anything to reassure us. She simply led them right to the door, and then walked off.

I'll say one thing. They didn't have anything personal against us. They just had a problem: If you have trapped gophers, white rats, or young ladies in a shed, how can you get to them without tearing up the door, which Mary Jane won't go for?

They never even talked about us as people. They talked about the garden hose. If they sent the garden hose in under the door, what would that do? If—no, they couldn't rock it. Dexter Point does not build potting sheds the way the rest of humanity does.

They looked at the door again. Mary Jane was firm about the door, so they left it on its hinges. When Mary Jane was convinced it was not going to be butted in, she consented to go somewhere with Jerry. Then the masterminds were left alone again.

One guy, when he was checking the door for the tenth time to see if it was still bolted, said, "Hey, you guys, I'm gonna make sure they don't escape while we're getting ready." He laughed a thick, heavy, almost moronic, laugh while he clamped the padlock shut on the door outside.

At last Johnny had an original idea. "Hey, we could smoke them out."

Part of me could not believe this was happening. I saw them get the wooden panels that fit up over the windows, and I felt the darkness thicken as they clamped them in place on the two shed windows. I heard them talking about needing to stuff something under the door and to make sure it didn't get pushed out again.

I don't even think they totally remembered why they were doing these things anymore. They just moved swiftly and logically from one step to the next. If Cris and I had offered to come out at that moment to save them all the trouble, I don't think the offer would have been accepted.

I asked myself, "What would Jason do? What would nine Jasons do?" I knew we had to get out of there in the next five minutes or forget it.

Oh, Lord, I found myself saying. Then I stopped. *That's right,* I thought. *The Lord!* I felt a strong urge to find Cris. It was so dark with the window panels up, you couldn't see anything. Finally I touched her dress. "Cris," I said. "We have to pray, and then we have to get out of here."

"OK," she said.

"Dear Lord," I said. "Cris and I need you real bad. . . ."

There was a heavy, powerful presence in the shed. Cris and I could both feel it. Something inside me told me I had to say, "I put this into your hands, Lord. No matter what happens, we are going to trust you, Lord. Right, Cris?"

Cris squeezed my hand. It was solemn and deep and almost thrilling.

My wits cleared then, and I remembered the little walkway at the back of the potting shed. There was a sliding accordion door that opened into the greenhouse part. Cris and I eased our way through it, and we crawled on our stomachs to the back of the greenhouse.

There was some kind of covering on the greenhouse, too. It was totally dark in there except for a little patch of light here and there. You could only see shapes. Inside the whole thing was made of this kind of heavy plastic. I kicked my foot against one pane of it. Nothing.

Then I remembered the weed puller. I didn't want to, but I forced myself to crawl back into the potting shed and find the weed puller. I was less sure now that I would not use the spray. So I weakened and took it along.

Outside the guys were stuffing things under the door and talking about the best kinds of torches. It was like a nightmare, but really more like a dream, now that we were doing something.

"Whatever happens from all of this, Lord; whatever it is, I'm going to trust you," I muttered as I crawled back through the walkway.

9
ESCAPE

It seemed like all the weed puller did was scratch the plastic. I couldn't even make a dent in the stuff. Then finally I got smarter; I put the weed puller in the corner of one of the sections and started trying to break and pry the corner out of the molding.

I heard one of the boys in the front say, "Get some gas from the lawn mower!" real loud to someone evidently further away. I also heard a scream now and then and some music.

I think I might even have forgotten to be quiet if it hadn't been for Cris. She was so quiet. She sat nearby, supporting me as a friend but saying nothing. It was strange after all these times when Cristella had been my help that now she needed me.

Every so often when I would lean back to push

the hair out of my eyes, I would get a terrible feeling that I can't quite describe. Suddenly I seemed to sense that I was trapped. Then the air inside the greenhouse seemed to be all used up, and I would feel that I had to get out that instant.

By now you could hear that the guys were moving into their plan. "Not that way, dang it!" one said. "Are you trying to kill me?"

Good question, I remember thinking.

Finally I got a little nick to fit the weed puller in, and I pried with all my might. Nothing. I did it about three times; then finally the weed puller began to bend. It was getting bent rather than gouging out the plastic. I can tell you right now that anybody who wanted the world's greatest greenhouse should go to that company.

I pulled the weed puller all the way through and began kind of sawing with it, pulling with all my might to make the crack bigger. Then I got the idea of pushing and pulling with it back and forth, like a lever on an outboard motor. The weed puller was bending, but so was the plastic.

When I could, I grabbed a little section of the plastic with my hand (I still have a little scar there where it cut me) and pulled it towards me while I pushed against the rest of it with my feet. This feeling was coming over me again that there was no air in that greenhouse. I felt nausea and terror pouring over me.

Then, before I realized it, there was a feeling of calm coming over me. At first I thought it might be, you know, Anjie, or something because it was so different from how I'd been feeling. But it wasn't Anjie. It was a feeling that we would get out of there soon, but that was all. I never felt like "Everything will be all right," just "We will get out of here soon." So I stopped feeling quite so terrified and began to pull with my hands and the weed puller and push with my feet.

Finally, Cris stirred. "Let me pull," she said. She seemed to feel better when she began to work on it, too. I knew how hard it was, and I didn't want her to tear her hands, but we couldn't think about that now. Suddenly a bigger piece of the plastic began to bend—up higher than I expected it to, like something had suddenly ripped loose up there.

We pulled the plastic toward us, but we couldn't let go of it to crawl through the opening it made. There was a tarp of some kind over the greenhouse. We'd have to crawl through the plastic, and then find a wide-enough opening to go under the tarp.

"Dave!" I heard suddenly, when I pried back the plastic with Cristella's help. "That stupid thing's caught on, down there in the corner. It's going, man!"

I looked over my shoulder. It was dark, but it wasn't as dark as it should have been. Then I got a deep breath of smoke.

"Cris, they've got it on fire!"

Then Cristella said an amazing thing. "I've got to go back and shut that door."

"What door?"

"That door into the greenhouse," she said, and she dropped down to crawl back toward it.

"No, Cris, Please. Please don't," I said. "There's stuff we don't know, and, please. I'll do anything, only please."

She stopped. She turned suddenly and grabbed the plastic right up above where my hands were. She pulled. And I pulled. I do not know how she managed, but she pulled that thing so far that I could squeeze my upper body between the plastic and the tarp. I braced my body against it and held it.

"Crawl past my legs," I said.

"Where?" she said. Then she found the opening by my feet and squirmed down into it. My face was up against the tarp, and I was trying not to gag or scream. I had sweat running down my back; both my arms and my legs were shaking. I thought if I didn't get that tarp away from my face, I just wouldn't make it.

Cris picked up the weed puller as she crawled through. She ran it along the bottom of the tarp until she found a stake. Then she crawled over on the other side of it. "Reach down and grab the bottom of the tarp in your hands," she said.

It was hard because the plastic was cramping me into the tarp, but I did it. "Pull up with all your strength," she said.

I pulled. She pulled. The stake was at an angle toward us so it didn't give up right away. When I thought I couldn't pull anymore, it finally came away.

Cris and I put our faces on the ground and looked out into fresh air. We were so tired we both just wanted to sit there and breathe and look at the stars and feel the cold on our arms. I knew we couldn't do that, though.

It sounded like everybody in the world was in front of the potting shed. "Get that so-and-so hose over here!" one guy was saying. "I don't want to go to jail, man!"

"Will you get the other end of that stupid hose connected, dummy!" the first one yelled. "Mary Jane is going to see this so-and-so fire in a minute, man, and then we have had it."

"I say let's get out of here, now!" another one said.

"Oh, sure! They don't have any idea who we are, now do they? You idiot." Flames were visible from where we were, but we were not exactly in their line of sight.

"Cris, we've got to get out of here," I whispered. "Let's go over that fence real quiet. On the other side, down some ways, is the ocean, I think."

Cris was cold and scared and brave. She picked up the weed puller and walked over to the side fence, furthest away from the boys. Without saying a word, she grabbed her skirt and tucked it up into her waistband on one side. Then she pulled herself over the fence. I did the same. It was scratchy, and the top of each board was pointed so my own weight was driving the point into my stomach. I finally got to the other side, but my dress was torn right in the middle. I had splinters in my legs. My

73

hands were cut and bruised from the plastic. I wondered why I couldn't see anything. Then I realized I had had my eyes shut ever since I got on top of the fence.

When I looked around, it was confusing. There was no path, just shrubs and clumps. There was a little downward slant to the ground though.

"It's down this way," I said, precisely because I didn't know which way it was, I guess. Sometimes you just have to do it, no matter.

The swearing and the bickering and the flames and the yelling were suddenly joined by screams and high-pitched shrieking.

"Come on, Cris!" I said. We both pitched and slipped and slid and ran and staggered down the hill. Now that I was breathing fresh air again, it seemed to me that everything was bound to turn out right.

Don't ask me how we finally found the beach. It turned out to be not only down a little slanted hill, but then there was a drop-off kind of hill, and we clutched and clawed and crawled and half-plunged and fell down it. If I could have seen half of what we were doing, I would have died where I was.

By the time we reached the flat, we were freezing and exhausted and starving all at once. But it was so peaceful. We could hear the ocean and see the waves further out in the skinny moonlight. But where we were it was quiet and completely private. We kept walking. I knew what general direction we should be going from Dexter Point, but I didn't have any idea how far we would have to go to get back to town.

Now that we were away from Mary Jane and her "gentle companions" as the romantics would say, I began to feel better.

Cristella brightened up considerably. "I don't think Johnny is really my type," she laughed. "But if you like him, Angie, I think I could fix you up."

"Oh, I've been fixed up," I said. "Evidently you didn't notice my new dress." I twirled. "I spent nearly two hours getting fixed up. Can't you tell?"

"I'm sorry your dress is ruined, Angie. It is pretty," she said. "It might be sewed."

I felt wonderfully happy and wild and witty. "Oh, no, it's my own fault," I said. "I got everything backwards. It's my new pajamas that are fireproof. At the other parties I've been to, we nevah, nevah set firah to the buildings until we're all ready for bed."

We both laughed and laughed. It felt so good and so right to be bouncing along the beach, larking around. Cristella giggled. "Oh, you know, I did leave a few things at Mary Jane's. Do you have time to walk me up there to get them?"

We laughed again. "Why, naturally," I said. "Only I don't think it's good manners to drop in so late. Why don't we send our Cadillac around in the morning?"

"Good idea." I could see Cristella's eyes sparkling as she agreed. "My pajamas are green, so send the green one. Whatever you do, don't send the pink one."

I can't remember all the nonsense we talked coming down to the village from the point. But we were in high spirits by the time we reached our blocks.

Then I had a great idea. "Crissy, are you dead, dead tired?"

"Why?"

"I've got four dollars in my box at home. We could go in real quiet, and I could get it, and we could go down to Mindy's on the bus and get some fish and chips. Want to?"

She did. I slipped into the house, and everyone was sound asleep. I loved them so much as I walked to my room. I grabbed two coats for me and Cris, got the four dollars, and left. By the time we caught the bus, it was fifteen minutes until twelve.

When we slid into the booths, it was almost 12:20. Hardly anyone was there, and the air smelled warm and greasy.

Mindy's is just as you get into the university district. It's old and full of posters and printed announcements, and there's always newspapers lying around and some students studying in the corners. Of course, I had never been there at that time of night before, but I knew it would be open.

We sat for a few minutes and read the menu. We decided on about fifteen different things. Then we tried to see how many things we could get for $3.20, which is what I had left. Just as we had it all figured out, we remembered we had to have bus fare back, so we had to start all over again.

At 12:30, the news came on. Cris and I were sitting with our heads resting on our arms on the table, waiting for our order. We were as happy as we had ever been in our lives, even though everything was bonkers.

"Once again tonight, truth and tragedy have proven to be stranger than fiction," the newscaster announced. "There was a strange red glow in the Dexter Point residential area tonight. Some teenagers, evidently carried away with the fun of the moment, inadvertently set fire to a greenhouse in the back of the Knutsen residence on Dexter Point Drive. Two teenagers were believed to be trapped inside. Because of the possibility of smoke inhalation, the fire department sent its resuscitator unit to the scene of the fire—its only unit, since Dexter Point and environs are still unincorporated, and their fire department is locally staffed and equipped.

"There are people who don't believe in fate. This item is for them. By a strange, shall we call it, 'coincidence,' that resuscitator was needed elsewhere in that suburb tonight. A five-year-old boy, Ramon Mendez, with a congenital heart defect—one of thousands of so-called "blue babies," died at 11:05 tonight on his way to the hospital while the ambulance, which might have saved his life, was racing to rescue *his sister, Cristella Mendez*, one of the guests at the Knutsen party. We will have more details at the . . ."

I could not move. By the time the announcer said, "Ramon," Cristella had simply vanished. She

streaked out the door, and I sat stupidly and
watched her. She ran across the street, and I saw
her for a moment only. She had bumped or been
bumped by a car coming to a stop. He honked and
honked. Then I saw her pick herself up and keep
running.

Someone in the restaurant was screaming.
"Jesus, you didn't! You wouldn't! I hate you!"

It was me.

10
GRADY

It's confusing to me how I finally ended up at the infirmary, which is really for college students. They put me there, though, and when I woke up, mom was there. She never said one thing. Her eyes were horrible, like a war refugee. She just laid her face against my blanket and sat there. I felt groggy and didn't much care who was there and who wasn't. It was all like it wasn't true anyway.

Later I woke up and my dad was there. I was surprised to see him, but I was so tired I just looked at him and tried to concentrate on what he was saying.

He looked very uncomfortable, and he was saying some strange things, I thought. He said, "How's it going?" Then later on he said, "We're going to have a talk when you're feeling better. I have some things I want to tell you."

I said "OK," but then he didn't come back for two days.

That infirmary. I knew I was really weirded out or something, but I couldn't make my thoughts work right. Just when I'd get everything laid out in my mind just the way it was; then something would mix it all up. Just like if you had all the pattern pieces for about forty-four blouses laid out on the fabric but not pinned, and then the wind blew through.

None of my thoughts were about the party or anything. You know, about that night. Not then. Only about other things. I mean, really dumb things. Like, did Merced really have five kittens after all? Jason said she had five but she ate one. In my dream mom said, "Jason! Don't say things like that!" But she never said if it was true or not.

Then I got to thinking I had left that silly poem about Mrs. Rohrbaugh in my desk, and if anybody looked in my desk for anything, she would find it. I wanted to have someone I could trust go and get in my desk and get that poem out. But I couldn't think of anyone to ask.

So I'd sleep and sometimes I'd watch tv. People are forever getting cars for different things on television during the day. In one show, you answered all the questions; then you got the car keys. But there were five cars there, and to get the car, you had to pick out the right one. For some reason, that show made me furious. I wanted to call the emcee and tell him how unfair that was.

"He's answered all your dumb questions. Now you give him the car," I wanted to say.

I mean, really. I don't know why it mattered all that much.

Finally, my dad came again. He said he wanted me to get plenty of rest. He wouldn't say when he was coming back though. Sometimes he does that. You ask him a question, and he keeps talking to you; but he doesn't answer your question, and he knows he's not answering it, too. He brought me a Nancy Drew book, which I already had, but he didn't know that. I read it again.

Nobody said anything to me about why I was there. Nothing at all. They just kept telling me to get rest. I can get really rested after about five hours of sleep if my mind is working right. But there I was always sleepy. I wasn't too clear. I even swallowed the pills they gave me, which I never do.

Finally, one day I woke up. I laid there, and I could not remember some things. I couldn't exactly figure out why I was there or what illness I had. And there was something very important about a pair of green pajamas, but I was wearing a hospital gown and it was blue gray. Then I got some screwball notion that my family was moving while I was in the hospital, and when I came out, I wouldn't know where they lived.

All these things are all fine now. But I couldn't

turn loose of them then.

On the third day I met Grady. He was the staff counselor in the infirmary. That afternoon I opened my eyes, and this man was there. He seemed to bulge everywhere. His chest and arms bulged in his shirt, his neck bulged in his collar, and his eyes bulged in his head. I mean, I don't hate him or anything, but it just so happened that Grady looked that way.

He sat down on the foot of my bed, which the nurse had told my mom not to do. He had one of those fingernail clippers that shoot the clippings about ten feet sometimes.

"Angie?" he said, smiling. "Hi. My name is Grady. I'm a counselor here at the infirmary, and sometimes I work at a center across town. I thought maybe we could rap a little." He smiled again and clipped a piece of thumbnail.

You may as well know that my dad thinks counselors are "a bunch of fatheads that don't even know George is dead." I only knew George was dead from hearing my dad say that, but it always tickled me when he said it. He sounded so disgusted it would strike me funny.

Anyway, Grady wasn't terrible or anything. He liked to talk about feelings. Sometimes we have angry feelings, and sometimes we have happy feelings. We feel guilty for some of our feelings, but Grady thinks we shouldn't. We should get in touch with our feelings instead.

I couldn't really think of much to say to him. I finally told him about Merced's kittens and also about the poem I was afraid I had left in my desk. He didn't offer to get it or anything.

Instead, he told me that he wrote poetry, too. "Only," he said (sorta smugly I thought), "You wouldn't understand the poetry I write, I'm afraid."

Don't ask me why I said this, but it just came into my mind. "Don't you think that's kind of a romantic thing to say?" Mrs. Rohrbaugh said the romantics were very big on having nobody know what they meant.

But Grady! He about dropped his clippers.

"Romantic!" he said. "You thought I was trying to be romantic?" He rolled and unrolled one of his sleeves. I knew I had kinda fouled up, but I knew I couldn't fix it. I just wanted him to go.

"Tell me, Angie," he said, "do you have many boyfriends at school?"

See, that's what Mrs. Rohrbaugh says people always start thinking about when you say romantic. But I had forgotten. I just looked at him and before I could think about it, I blurted out, "Maybe you *don't* know George is dead." Soon as I said that I knew I shouldn't have. I didn't feel well enough to explain my dad's joke about counselors. For one thing, I was too groggy from the medicine they had given me.

Grady said, "Who? George? Was George your boyfriend?" Now this gets hard to understand, I know, because I wasn't feeling well. I started to laugh because of the joke, but then I started to cry. I couldn't stop myself. I cried and cried, and I was shaking the bed and digging into the pillow.

I knew it was something about being dead. It wasn't George, and it wasn't Merced's kitten. But someone knew who it was—a girl. "Anjie!" I cried, and I began to beg Grady to please leave and get my mom.

Now if I had been at home, everything might have been all right. Mom would have helped me remember about Ramon, and we could have faced that awful night together. But Grady didn't understand. He hadn't understood anything.

Instead he left, and I ended up going to the center. Grady told my mom that in his opinion I was "disturbed." That seemed to me to be such a nothing word.

I thought of a joke about that. I thought, *If Grady thinks that I'm disturbed, maybe the cure is a Do Not Disturb sign.* From me to Grady.

My dad came back the night before I went to the center. I couldn't believe how glad I was to see him and how handsome he was. He looked like— perfect. I wanted to tell him the joke (my dad loves jokes) about Grady and George and the romantics and all; but I was afraid I would start crying again, and then my dad would think I was crazy.

I didn't want people to think that. If they start thinking of you in that way, everything you say can come out to seem wrong.

Anyway, when my dad used to come into my room at night and sit on the edge of my bed for a few minutes, we always prayed. So, when he sat down on my bed that night—well, there it was. It was like we both knew the other one was remembering all those times.

"Your mom says you're going over to the K. T. Center," he said.

It's really hard to talk to someone when you're both thinking about something else, I've noticed. "Dad, you know there's this show on tv where they give away cars? Well, do you think it's fair if a guy answers all the questions right to make him miss his car, because he can't guess which car the keys belong to? See, they give the winner these keys, and there are five cars sitting there . . .?"

My dad said, "How's your mom been doing? Is she OK?"

"Yeah. I don't know. We were going to do some things to my room, but now we might not. Do you have a good place to stay, dad?"

"It's all right. It's not much really. What about Jason? What's he up to?"

"Well, I think he, you know, wishes it was time for you to move back and all. His bike chain fell off, but he thought he could fix it. He might have made it worse, though. I think he did."

Dad grinned kind of sadly. "Probably did, huh? How's Shelley? Is she growing?"

"Oh, yeah. She's growing a lot. You might not be able to tell because she's still small, but . . ."

Then he said "Angie?"

"Yeah?"

"I don't know much about that center, but I want to ask you. Do you think your mind is OK? I mean, can you think straight or are you confused?"

"I think I'm going to be OK. In fact, I am already. I'm a little tired tonight, but I think by tomorrow I will feel fine. Sometimes it seems like there's another girl—I mean, her name is Angie, too, of course (only I spell it *Anjie* to keep them straight) who wants to take over. She doesn't care about anything. But . . ." My dad looked so sick and hurt. He looked like he was poisoned almost. "But I'm not going to let her. Don't worry, dad. I'm going to keep on being me."

He looked at me for a long time. "Do you ever pray anymore, Angie?"

"Well, I did. But, no, I guess I don't now." I didn't remember right then why I was so emphatic about this.

My dad sat there just like he always did when he sat on my bed. "Do you think you'd be willing to pray with me, Ang? Just to ask God to keep you safe over at the center?"

There was a cold spot in my heart. Something I didn't want to remember had turned me stony towards God. But towards my dad, at that moment—well, I think if he had asked me to play "Wild Geese" on the clarinet I would have tried it.

It was quiet and heavy. There was a sorrow between us that was like the world's worst good-bye. We sat for several minutes with our hands together and our eyes closed, saying nothing. It was like we were in the grip of a powerful force in the room, something you could almost swim in.

"Dear Lord," my dad said and he stopped. After quite a while he went on. "I know you have some differences with me, Lord, but you can't possibly have anything against Angie."

Something uneasy stirred in my stomach. It seemed to me like Jesus probably could have, but I wasn't real specific about what it was.

There was a long silence. My dad was squeezing on my hands as though he was trying to hold on tighter and get away at the same time. I opened my eyes for a moment, and it seemed like he was trying to say something he could not bring himself to say. He let out a very long breath and a shudder went through him.

He was choking when he finally spoke, breathing hard, as though he was almost angry. "You fix Angie up, will you, Jesus? Get her thinking back where it belongs and make her heart so this other girl who wants to take over can't ever get in, Lord. You do that for us, and you can send me the bill. Whatever it is." He spit out those last words like his teeth were clenched against them, but he was determined to say them. Then he repeated it, but this time he sounded exhausted and quiet. "You send me the bill, Jesus. Even if it's . . . that."

I felt all the tension go out of my dad as I said my prayer. I asked God to bless everyone in our family and Naples and Merced and to help us get over our trial separation. He kissed my forehead and smiled at me before he left. He looked almost as if he had been crying.

The next morning I went to the center.

11
THE LORD

By now I think you know enough about the center. Like my dad says, "If that's the center, I'd hate to see the margins!" Mom asked me if I didn't think Dr. Hirschmann was "really quite nice"? How anyone can think Dr. Hirschmann is nice, and then not be able to see what I see in the Mendezes. . . . Anyway, I could tell by her voice she wasn't too sold on him, either.

One good thing happened to me while I was at the center. It was my dad's prayer; that's what he and I think now. Anyway, the second day I was in the center, something happened. You were supposed to get up and make your bed, and then go out and wander around in the halls and in the dayroom all day except for meals and grounds (going outside to this fenced area around the center).

That second morning I had to get out of my room. After all, I'd done nothing but sit in that room the first day. I went down the halls and looked in to see how people made their beds and stuff. I mean there was not much to do. There was a Ping-Pong table and a pool table, but no one wanted to play, and I felt funny fooling around with that cue stick. I don't really know how to play pool just right.

Anyway, I came to this one area. It turns out it was an area where people put their children while they visit people at the center. Right in the middle of all the toys was a trike exactly like Ramon's.

I looked at that trike and wanted to remember everything, and at the same time I didn't. I was shaking, and I felt cold and weak. Then, suddenly, I felt like the Lord was there. He was so very, very careful—like a person opening a very precious package. With me! Just me. I was the package. And inside was just about the world's greatest prize, according to him. And I was the prize. It was like I couldn't stand it, how careful he was being. Even if he had accidentally wrecked the package (which he never would) or ruined the prize, it was still unmistakable how he felt about it. How he felt about me. He knew it was only me, too.

I kept looking at the trike without moving. Just standing there with the Lord. Very carefully, in ways that are hard to explain, he showed me, by the trike being there and by the way the trike made me feel, that he loved Ramon as much as me.

We just stood there loving Ramon together. We

started with his delicate, dusty brown feet strapped on those trike pedals with two thick rubber bands crossed so his feet wouldn't fall off when Crissy pushed him.

Then I saw his tummy—round and smooth. When he was a little younger, Crissy used to bury her face in it and blow against it to make a kind of motorboat sound and make him squeal and giggle.

Finally I saw his eyes. When he was thinking his eyes looked far away, but Cris could always shine them up and make them dance with her teasing. In my thoughts, his eyes looked at me that way. Then I thought, *No, he's looking at Cris.* But his eyes insisted. They were looking at me shiny and dancing, too.

Then it was like the Lord looked at me. I thought, I won't be able to stand this, but I couldn't move. He looked at me, just like Ramon did—his eyes full of love. Suddenly something shifted in me. I knew I was different. It was Anjie. She was gone. I knew it.

It was as if she weighed a little bit, about a pound or so, and I felt her leave. It was also like she was torn loose, and I felt a stabbing. It wasn't killing or anything, but it was so sudden, I moaned a little before I knew it.

All at once there was a nurse there, and she said, "I'm supposed to get you back in your room so you can rest for a couple of hours before afternoon session."

As far as I know, no one ever got back into their room until after dinner except me—that day. She didn't even know why I was supposed to, but believe me, I wanted that two hours as much as I ever wanted anything.

When I woke up, they let me call my mom— which they also didn't want you to do for the first seventy-two. That's what they call, "the critical period"—the first seventy-two hours you are at the center. Personally, I don't think people mean to be necessarily critical. It's just not a great place.

All I wanted to ask mom was one question: "Where was Ramon?" meaning where were they putting him.

Mom kinda caught her breath because no one had talked to me about the Mendezes since that night. She said Ramon was buried in a cemetery about two miles from our house, but they were having a memorial service for him on Saturday afternoon. Then the nurse said they needed the phone back.

That's when I made up my mind. I had to get out of that center and go to the service. It was more important than breathing in and out, for my money.

When mom came to get me, it was Friday afternoon.

Being back home with Jason and Shelley and mom, and having everyone sort of act like normal more or less, made it hard to have memorial-service feelings when Saturday afternoon came around. It seemed odd to be dressed up, gloves and all, right in the middle of the afternoon.

I was trying to feel sorrowful, but I hoped Ramon

91

was not able to read thoughts now that he was in heaven. What I really wanted to do when I was walking across the church parking lot was to go horseback riding with Cristella. Of course I knew she never would. I'm just being honest, because you know I loved Ramon.

When I came in the church, it was dark and cool and quiet, and the usher was very solemn, taking me to a seat. I thought he might know what a good friend I was of Cristella's and Ramon's, and thinking how sad that might make him feel, made me feel a little tragic, I guess.

Pretty soon, there was a little flurry, and I turned around and it was like someone socked me right in the heart. It was Cristella and Miguel with Mr. and Mrs. Mendez. As soon as I saw them, I understood how shallow I had been feeling.

Every one of them looked so thin inside their clothes, and their eyes were full of hurt—but quiet. When I saw Cristella I felt willing, I really did, to be dead instead of Ramon. But then she and Ramon would be sad for me, and someone would have to take my place. Then someone would be sad for the people who lost them and on and on.

Cristella looked like she belonged in a hospital bed with one of those upside-down bottles dripping into her arm.

I thought about Ramon again through Cris's eyes. Imagine how Cris's face would change if Ramon would suddenly come into the room and say, "Where am I?"

He wouldn't though. He was gone. Worms

would eat him. I tried to hold back that picture, but I couldn't. No. Not the worms. Jesus, I pleaded. Please, another picture.

I wondered how worms ate, anyway. It seemed like they didn't have any mouths. I mean, where are their mouths? There's a cartoon worm at Maxie's with an engineer hat on, and he is talking with his mouth open. I couldn't remember whether he had teeth or not. Anyway, he wasn't real.

Then I remembered another funny thing. I am not afraid of worms really. I would rather sleep with fourteen worms than be in the room with one spurty-walking spider. Yuk.

Suddenly I realized Ramon was cold. If Crissy buried her face in Ramon's soft little belly, it would be cold. And stiff. I shuddered. My hands were getting sweaty, but I was getting cold myself.

I thought of Ramon lying in the ground. Then I thought of Jesus. He wouldn't want Ramon to be there. He loved Ramon. We had loved him together that day at the center. Jesus loved all of us so much he was crucified and rose from the dead—so none of us would die and remain in the ground.

Suddenly I realized Ramon wasn't there. The part of him that laughed and thought and felt—his spirit—was with Jesus. He was OK. And he was warm. He could see Crissy and he loved her; and he saw me, but he wasn't sorry he had died. He was OK.

I wanted to be sitting by Cristella and squeezing

her hand to let her know we would always be friends. Then Cristella would smile at me, and I would feel better.

"Hello, Angie," a voice said. I saw a soft, blue dress sit down by me, and a hand I'd seen before reached out and patted my knee. I looked up and jumped before I could stop myself. Mrs. Rohrbaugh. Honest to gosh, Mrs. Rohrbaugh, sitting down next to me and patting me. I couldn't say anything.

"Friends," said a voice in a microphone. A man had suddenly appeared on the podium. Then he looked around and put his microphone down. There weren't enough people there to bother with it, I guess.

"We are here to remember Ramon Mendez and to comfort and support the Mendez family in their loss." Everything got super quiet. "Let us pray."

The man began to talk to the Lord, and I knew right away that they were good friends. Somehow that made him my friend, too. He and Jesus and I and Cristella were very good friends. And Ramon. Ramon was with Jesus. Maybe riding on his shoulder like the picture of the lamb in the Good Shepherd picture. We were all friends.

And Mrs. Rohrbaugh. It was like a voice in my heart. I knew as sure as I'm saying this that Jesus was insisting that Mrs. Rohrbaugh be mentioned in the friendship circle. I wasn't too sure, but it was like I promised to think about it. That didn't seem to be good enough.

Finally I kind of whispered, "Okay. She can."

That was all. But a weight lifted off me, and by then the man's prayer was over.

Now he talked a little about death. I was thinking about Cristella mostly, and then suddenly, there she was, up on the podium standing beside the man. The man said each person would say a few words about Ramon.

Cristella's voice sounded like dust almost, but somehow she could be heard. For one thing, everyone was riveted to what she was saying.

"Ramon was my brother and my friend. He was very good to animals and to our kittens. He could hold them without squeezing them. Also, he was easy to teach things. He could write the alphabet and his name." Her voice quavered a little. In fact, her voice was so small already it almost went away. But it didn't. She went on.

"He could count to thirty-nine." She stopped again, and I felt the tears spill over my eyes like a flood. "His favorite story was *Jack and the Beanstalk*. See, he wanted mama to buy a cow so he could trade her for some beans."

Boy, I think everybody was crying by then, and they didn't care if it showed or not. "I think Ramon could have been a doctor or the president someday. . . ." She stopped again, but then quickly finished. "Because he had so much about him that was special."

Then Miguel stood up. He said that Ramon liked cowboys, especially the bad guys. There was a slight ripple of gentle laughter. Then he said, "I think he might have liked some of the good guys, too, but I'm not sure." Then he added, "Yeah, he did."

He sat down and Mrs. Mendez stood. Without moving to the podium, she turned and faced everyone. "When you live with a child every day, every day, you know that you love him. When he is taken away, you know that that love will always be a part of you."

Mr. Mendez thanked everyone for coming and invited them to come to his home anytime. "We are grateful you have come here," he said. "My family and I are grateful."

Another prayer was said and everyone stood. I started down the aisle; then I remembered that I had promised the Lord that Mrs. Rohrbaugh would be a part of the friendship circle. I didn't know what to do, but it seemed like my heart was going to burst wide open with sadness and gladness at the same time.

It probably sounded dumb, but I just blurted out, "Cristella is exactly what she said about Ramon."

Mrs. Rohrbaugh looked at me with her full attention, and she looked so different than she ever had before. More loving or something. So I just said, "She could be anything, Mrs. Rohrbaugh. Even a ballerina, I'll bet. Good-bye."

I don't know if she was going to say anything or not. I just knew I had to get outside so I could breathe. I pushed the side door open real fast and almost fell down the stairs onto Seneca Street.

12
OSTRICHES

There are two things about the trial separation I will never forget, and both of them are dinners.

First of all, my Grandfather Ahearne came to see us on Memorial Day weekend. He does not like to take trips anymore, but he came anyway—all the way from Idaho.

He is a super grandfather, but it is not exactly "fun city" when he is angry. He does not lose his temper when people spill things or knock them over or when kids make noise.

But he gets angry when people know what is right and do wrong. If that happens to be you, keep moving—that's my advice. Dad has always said, "If Jesus wants a popgun, he sends Birdie (that's my grandma); but if God needs a cannon, he sends Omar (Grandpa Ahearne).

When everybody heard that grandpa was coming, something began to happen to our whole family. It was as if we all began holding our breath simultaneously. I guess I mostly mean dad and mom and me. Jason and Shelley were interested, of course, but they didn't know really. Something told me, though, my prayers about the trial were to be answered soon.

That's not what my dad said though. In fact, he didn't say anything about it. Mom had me call him at work to tell him Grandpa Ahearne was coming.

He said, "Did your mom ask him to?"

I said, "No. She's trying everything to get the house ready, because she didn't know."

"Put your mom on the phone, please."

I heard her talk then: "I did not. No, I did not. The only time I talked to Birdie was when Angie was in the infirmary. I told her as little as possible, but I asked her to pray.

"Yes, I think she did find out that you were not living here—but that was from Jason, not from me.

"No, I was not going to tell your own children to lie for you. You're not afraid she'll worry. You're afraid she'll pray."

Mom told dad the night they were supposed to arrive, and invited him to his own home for dinner the following night. He said he'd come.

That's when I got my idea. I decided to ask him to come to dinner on Father's Day, and I would cook the meal. Me and the kids. That's the second dinner I want to tell you about, but first you need to know about grandma and grandpa.

My mom was not sitting around the house shivering in a sweater at this point. As soon as we heard grandma and grandpa were coming, our house almost lost its whole personality from trying to stay so clean. I couldn't even keep any socks in the dirty clothes. Whop! Back they came to my drawer before my shoes even missed them. My room was the only place that still looked kind of friendly.

Mom got a permanent and bought quite a few groceries. Jason and Shelley had to come to the table for everything they ate. Jason was supposed to eat with one hand in his lap all the time. That really got me, no lie.

Grandma and grandpa came one evening after dinner, and my dad stopped by for a few minutes and then left, and we all went to bed. The next day grandma and grandpa visited mom and us kids and dad worked. Then that night he came over for dinner after work, just like when he lived there.

My parents were so nervous it was making us all weird. My mom ate nothing. She said the turkey was not done. My dad kept on saying it was. Jason was feeding Naples at the table, and my mom was clearing her throat about ninety-three times to stop him. But he didn't get what she meant.

Grandma talked about a lot of people in Idaho that nobody knew. I thought it was kind of interesting, because you don't really have to know the exact person—you can still feel how glad they would be to grow dahlias the size of dinner plates or how sorry they'd be if their married son went bowling three nights a week with the grocery money. I was the only one who seemed to be listening, though.

Shelley was so upset because she couldn't sit in her regular place at the table and had to have a high chair that nobody right next to her could hear much anyway.

"Shelley, honey, it's OK," my mom said.

"You're making my ears blind, dummy!" said dear old guess who, and that upset my mom even more. But my dad laughed.

Grandpa said nothing. His face was like a founding-father picture. He went right through all the eating time, and everyone chattered and clattered and howled and squabbled and watched. And waited.

After everything was cleared except the dessert dishes, my grandfather lifted his eyes and looked at all of us. Then he looked at my father. I know for a fact if anyone ever looks at me that way I will shrivel to a pea, that's all I can say. I'd like to see old Hershey-Bershey get the gems out of grandpa's vault!

Everything got quiet. Shelley put her face down on the high chair and stuck her thumb in her mouth. Jason moved his chair over and put his head in grandpa's lap. Man! About any kid would curl up on grandma any day, but only Jason would plunk down on grandpa without even wondering if it was OK first.

"Lewis," he said finally, after it was so quiet you could hear the kittens moving around in their box. "Where are you sleeping nights?"

It was as if an electric shock went through the room. I couldn't move anything but my eyes.

My father said, "Sir?" very respectfully, and my grandpa repeated the question.

"I have a little room with a bath downtown during the tax season this year," my dad said. I felt sorry for him in a way. My grandpa spoke quietly but clear and firm, and every word was pronounced. His eyes gleamed like two little glinting fires. It made you shiver. I wanted to be on the same side as grandpa about everything. It seemed like you'd be more right and more safe and more respected and even more American or something.

My grandpa kept looking at my dad. "It's about three blocks from my office," my dad said, like he was trying to be very helpful.

"When exactly is 'tax season'?" grandpa said.

My dad started to answer; then he stopped. "I plan to keep the room for whenever I need it," he said. He was getting a little angry, but it was different than grandpa's anger. I guess you could say that my dad was losing his temper, and grandpa was using his.

"Need it for what?" grandpa asked, watching him.

"Whenever I have things to do in town," my dad said, trying to look at grandpa head-on, but not quite doing it.

"What are these things?"

"Oh, working late, seeing a movie, going to a ball game, maybe. I don't see where it needs to concern you," he said.

I could not believe my dad. He was more polite than he might be to most people who ask him questions. But how he could say anything even that strong to grandpa was beyond me.

Grandpa never batted an eye. "Are you telling me to mind my own business, son?"

"Well, I wouldn't want to have it sound . . ." my dad began.

"I hope you are telling me to mind my own business, Lewis. I hope you are."

A little thrill went down my back. My mom was sitting in the chair across from me, drawing on the tablecloth with her fork handle. I wanted to see her face, but I couldn't really.

"It's just that I'm not into hearing what you or anybody . . ." my dad began again.

"Not 'into hearing,' did you say?"

"Yes, sir."

"I thought that's what you said." My grandfather was glowering now but only with his eyes and eyebrows. "Well, I suggest you get 'into hearing' as you call it. Because I'm into telling you. In fact," grandpa pulled a watch out of his pocket, looked at it, clicked it shut, and put it away again.

"I have come 2,300 miles to tell you this. It's about ostriches, Lewis. I came to tell you about female ostriches." My father was looking at grandpa now. It was like he couldn't help it.

"The Bible says that ostriches leave their eggs in the earth and warm them in dust, forgetting that feet may crush them or wild beasts may break them. It says that ostriches are hardened against their young ones, as though they didn't belong to them.

"All the labor of a female ostrich is in vain, Lewis, because they do not have fear. Because God has deprived them of wisdom and has not given them any understanding.

"You know what I'd do if I were a female ostrich, Lewis?" grandpa asked.

My father cleared his throat. "No, sir."

"Oh, I beg your pardon," grandpa said. His eyes were like blazing, piercing lights looking at my dad. "I thought you did know. Yes, sir, I thought you knew. Well, sir, if I were a female ostrich I would do what the jackass does. I would get myself a little room with a bath in town, and I would leave my young ones out in the dust of the earth, as though they didn't belong to me, where they could be crushed or broken."

It was so quiet it was like death. But it was very exciting.

"Now in Bible times, course, they didn't use to rent rooms to ostriches and jackasses. But anymore, they do. In case they might want to go to a ball game or something of that nature."

My dad looked down at the table.

"And then I thought I'd tell you about my friend James. He's kind of a consultant, I guess you would say, on various matters. He's kind of a plain-talking fellow, which I appreciate. James, he had a friend in the tax business, I believe, Lewis, like yourself. James wrote Matthew and all his other friends a letter one time. It was a pretty good letter, most people think. At least they went and put it in the Bible.''

My grandpa reached in his inner coat pocket and brought out a little black New Testament that molded into his hand like wax.

" 'Matthew,' James wrote, 'God does not tempt people. So if you and the boys are looking to get tempted, then you will have to do it yourselves.'

" 'First off,' he said, 'you get yourself drawn away by your own lust until you reach the point of being enticed. Then you just leave it to lust.' Lust will conceive and bring forth sin, according to James. And when sin is finished, it will bring forth death.''

My dad was listening by this time. His eyes were glued to grandpa, and he wasn't saying a word.

"Personally, Lewis,'' he said slowly, "I don't have much of a taste for death. It always seemed like a pretty stringy old buzzard to me, somehow. However, I will say this. Some folks like it. Or seem to. And for those that do, why old James, he laid it right out for them.''

The phone rang two times then; and grandpa looked at it, and it stopped. I kid you not! I got little prickles all over my scalp. I mean the phone stopped ringing. I don't even think dad or mom noticed it.

"I thought we might take an example and see how James's idea might work,'' grandpa continued. "Let's take the death of this little Mendez boy, for instance. He died before his time, you might say. Now the ambulance that was to save his life was off somewhere else, I take it. Isn't that right, Angie?"

My name came very unexpectedly, but my grandpa was very gentle and kind when he looked at me. I couldn't speak, but I nodded yes.

"Now I couldn't rightly say what the ambulance was doing. Could have been hunting for some of those ostrich eggs that were left lying in the dirt for all I know. Or, I think somebody said that it was going to rescue some teenage girls who were being allowed to go off to a party no one knew very much about—same difference really.

"Now if James is right, and I think he is, it just could be that that jackass was led by his own lust and enticed. Then that lust brought forth lots and lots of sin. Lust is very fertile, I've noticed. Fact, it could well have been some of that very same sin that eventually caused that ambulance to be needed for those girls. Then sin, as you know, brings forth death."

My grandpa dropped his eyes and his voice for the first time.

"Course death doesn't confine his diet to ostriches and jackasses, like maybe it should. It takes what's made available. So now Ramon Mendez is dead."

A light turned on inside my head, like you sometimes see in cartoons. I saw how everything that had happened all fit together differently than I had thought it did.

All of a sudden I saw what grandpa saw: that the Lord could never be the one to blame for evil

105

things happening. It's us. In ways we don't expect, we get things started that we can't stop.

The Lord knew I had been angry at him, and he had arranged for me to understand. All this went through my head so fast, it was over before I really had a chance to think about it. But it cleared my head like a big sneeze.

My dad gave the table a shove and stood up angrily. He glared at grandpa. "Do you seriously mean to tell me you think that because I took a room in town I personally killed Ramon Mendez?!"

My grandpa looked real steadily at my dad. "Well, now, me and James don't decide any of the actual cases, of course. As I say, he's kind of a consultant and I'm . . . well, I'm just one of James's friends." Then grandpa looked up quickly. "There are courts that decide such things, however. Very high courts. Very stiff sentences. I can tell you one thing. I wouldn't want to be found guilty of contempt by those judges."

My dad threw on his coat and headed for the door. "Thanks for the dinner," he said. "Mom, I'm glad you could come out." He opened the door and looked back at my grandpa. See, my dad is my grandpa's only son, and the feelings between them "go very deep," grandma says. He looked at grandpa and started to speak, then turned to go again.

Grandpa leaned forward a little. "I'd get up and see you out, Lewis," he said, "but I have your little boy asleep on my lap. Seems like I'm in a regular way of minding your business, here lately. I had hoped I might get some pointers from you while I was here on how to mind my own business. But you got most of your business farmed out to me and your wife for the time being, I guess."

My dad slammed the door; then he slammed the car door; then he scattered gravel digging out.

Grandpa seemed cheerful and completely at ease about everything, but he did reach in his vest and take out a little pill he takes for his heart condition. He swallowed it with the rest of his water. Then he carried Jason to bed.

13
FATHER'S DAY

Two weeks before school was out, Cristella came back so she could finish up and graduate with her eighth-grade class. You cannot imagine how good it was to have her back. We just smiled at each other for about the first five minutes. Then we both started talking at once.

I told her about my plan to have dad over on Father's Day. Then she told me something that just about blew me away. She looked me right in the eye and she said, "Guess what we're going to do with Ramon's room, Angie."

I started to drop my eyes, but she wouldn't let me. She looked very insistently at me so I wouldn't. "Oh, what?" I finally said. My sandwich began to stick in my throat.

"We are going to paint it and make a divider in

the middle, and in August we are going to get two little foster kids from the Welfare Department—a brother and sister whose parents can't take care of them. They're Chicano, too."

At first I didn't have anything to say. Cristella mentioning Ramon was so sudden and now this. I just sat.

"You can help me fix the room if you want. And you can help teach them things, Angie. You can be kind of like their other sister, like you were with Ramon."

Can you believe that? I still couldn't answer her. Finally I said, "I'd like to," and I was suddenly so hungry to see all the Mendezes and get started with the room that I almost forgot my own plans.

Cristella didn't though. She said something else I wouldn't have thought of in a hundred years. "It's very brave to do what you're doing, Angie."

"What do you mean?" I said. "What are you talking about?" Man, I can't even kill a spider.

"To be trying to save your family. Trying to get everything right again." She smiled. "Like you saved me in the greenhouse."

"I saved you?" I remembered her telling me to grab the tarp and pull when I was about to pass out from horror.

"Of course you saved me," she said in a perplexed way as though she couldn't understand how I could have forgotten anything so important. "You pushed, you pulled, you prayed, you practically killed yourself tearing up the greenhouse while I sat there and shivered."

"Cris, you didn't. We both . . ."

"Oh, no. I finally pulled on the tarp a little bit, but it was you—you know that," she said as though she were scolding me ever so slightly for trying to lie my way out of it. "I am not a fighter like you are, Angie. In the good sense, I mean. I would never have gotten out of there." She paused. "And now you are fighting to save your family. If my father had moved out, I couldn't think of a single thing to do. But you—you have ideas. Like this Father's Day deal."

I do cry sometimes, as you know. So I guess you won't be too surprised if I tell you I just sat there. I put my hand over my mouth, and I could feel my eyes filling up. I just couldn't help it. It was only for a minute, and it was a good kind of crying. I just hadn't known anyone was noticing me in a special way.

It turned out that it was a very good thing Cristella said those things, though. Because the dinner was the hardest thing I've ever done. For a joke you could say, "The dinner was no picnic, believe me."

I was supposed to make the main dish, and Shelley and Jason were going to help with the rest. Shelley was going to make Jell-O, and Jason was going to make toast and fruit salad. I could make any main dish I wanted to, but it took me the longest time to decide. One thing I knew: Nothing we made in home ec. Eggs a la Goldenrod? Tuna Sorento? My dad would barf.

I just kept thinking: I can't give up, because Cris says I am a fighter. And the Lord. I knew he was wanting to be in on this. Some things I do might be kind of neutral, but I knew this was right and he would help me. Besides, I asked him to.

He's probably the one that gave me my great idea. I was getting very tired of my mom's drippy cookbook—with all the odd names like Lentil Lasagna and Filet of Sole Marguery. As I started to close the book, right out of nowhere I got my main idea. Bacon!

Bacon and toast and fruit salad and Jell-O and Kool-Aid and maybe a cake. See, when you have bacon for breakfast, everyone gets only about three pieces. But my idea was to have as much as anybody wanted.

At first I planned twenty-one pieces for everyone. It sounded right and besides, Father's Day was on the twenty-first of June. But then I thought maybe twenty-one for Shelley and Jason and twenty-five for everybody else. Shelley might only want ten, but if I fixed her twenty-one, dad and I could eat what she didn't want.

A real dinner needs a vegetable, so I thought we'd have french fries. I was going to make them myself, but the cookbook said to wash and peel the potatoes. Right there it didn't even make sense. Why would you wash them if you were going to peel them? Then it said to cut them "uni-formly."

I decided to buy french fries at the Dairy Queen. You can get quite a few for two or three dollars. I knew that Jason had five dollars, and mom would give us some.

There was one change. Jason would only give one dollar, and he wanted to make milk shakes instead of fruit salad. He claimed he had seen mom do it when I was at camp last year. So we changed. It was worth it to get Jason on our side. I knew if I started fighting with him, the Lord might scrap the whole plan.

Since Jason only gave one dollar, we decided to have tortilla chips for the vegetable. Bacon, toast, tortilla chips, Jell-O, and cake.

"Jesus," I said, "if you want to add something to this menu that will make dad decide the trial is over, be my guest." It's hard for me to imagine anymore how I used to think the Lord was so far away. He knew exactly what I said, and I'll prove it to you. But you have to have faith while it's going on—that's the thing.

Jason spent about the entire afternoon of Father's Day leaning against the couch looking out the window. At 4:45 he shouted, "Dad's here!" He bounded to the front door and threw it open. "Dad! Hi, dad! We're going to stand everyone at baseball with you and me on the same team. OK?"

Then Shelley hid behind the door. When daddy came through and reached around to shut the door, it wouldn't close and little squeals and giggles came from in back of it. Dad peered around behind it, and Shelley giggled and covered her eyes.

Dad reached down and grabbed her and hauled her over his head and she was squealing and giggling. Then, I'm sorry to say, she had a little accident. She sort of partly wet her pants (that's a problem with her sometimes), and a little bit of it splattered on dad's cheek and down his arm. That's when things began to go sour. Daddy frowned and set her down kinda fast.

"Still at that old stuff, huh?" he said with a little sigh of disgust. Shelley stood there, looking solemn as a cow, even after dad moved away. Finally, she walked very slowly into the bathroom and sat down on the throw rug with the door open, two fingers in her mouth and her other hand going round and round in her hair.

It made me feel sad, but I didn't want to do anything to make dad feel unwelcome.

Then Jason started. "Hey, dad, when are we going to play ball?"

"Oh, I don't know about that," dad said with a little smile on his face. He had come into the kitchen where mom and I were, and he was looking at mom.

"Come on, dad! Please. You can pitch or bat or anything. You can bat first, OK? Let's just you and me play."

My mom looked the way she does just before she gets headaches—like every little noise is almost a karate chop on her nerves. My dad doesn't like her to get headaches, so I hoped she wouldn't.

Jason was about to explode. "Can we play now, dad, and eat later? It's still light out and I have my mitt. Come on, dad, will you? I can catch really good now. Grounders! Really."

Dad sat with one hand in his lap (I had forgotten

how big he was) and his arm leaning on the table. He was listening to Jason, but his eyes were following mom around the room. He seemed to be waiting for her to say something.

Jason began to pull on dad's hand in his lap. "Come on, dad! Please. You can bat first and everything. OK?"

Dad still didn't say anything. It's like I told you. Sometimes he just won't answer.

Jason kept pulling and began yelling, "Dad! Will you? Just for a minute. Please. Dad!"

My mom was moving around the room a little in a real stiff way, like she was hardly alive.

I said, "Dad, we get to have all the bacon we want for dinner, and you get to have the most. You can have just as much as you want. Sometimes we just get three pieces, but tonight . . ."

Suddenly my mom whirled around and let me have it. "I'm sorry if the meals you get around here aren't adequate."

"Carolyn!" dad said. "Angie didn't mean that. She was just telling me about the dinner."

"Let's go, dad! Come on, while it's still light." Jason began thrusting his mitt up into dad's face. Dad warded it off by moving his head to one side and pushing the mitt away, but it was getting to him.

Then mom said, "I don't believe Angie needs anyone to come in here and explain to me what she means. She seems to be able to communicate the rest of the time."

Dad really got mad then, but it was Jason that got

it. "Can't you hush up for five minutes so we can hear ourselves think, Jason?" He suddenly freed the hand that Jason was pulling on and pushed the mitt and Jason away at the same time. Jason fell backward and landed in a heap against the kitchen cabinet. Mom shrieked, and I jumped, and my brother began to howl his head off.

"Oh, knock it off!" dad said. "You aren't really hurt." His howls inspired Shelley. Suddenly she began to scream so you could hear her three miles away.

It's hard to ignore all that stuff, but I knew I had to do something. I tried to get my dad's eye. "About how many pieces do you think you could eat, dad? I was going to fix you about twenty-one, but there's more . . ."

Then my mom looked right at dad. "It's such a comfort to have someone around who can interpret for all of us. Tell us what we mean by what we say, tell us whether we're hurt or not when we're hurled into cabinets, tell the baby what a failure she is when she has an accident sometimes . . ."

Now dad was really mad. "What do you expect, Carolyn? The kid wets in my face, this one is yanking my arm off and breaking my eardrum at the same time, and you and Angie have some deal going so no matter what I say about the bacon, it's going to be wrong! I shouldn't have come." He stood up suddenly.

"No, daddy. Don't go." I was starting to panic, so I had to say something. "We don't have to have bacon. Or we can have three pieces each, like

115

always. I don't even like it as much as I used to. Jason, stop yelling, right now! Shelley, close the bathroom door! OK?" My heart felt like it was going to come crashing through my chest any minute.

Dad brushed off his slacks and looked at mom. "I'm sure I've done some inexcusable wrong to everyone, but I just can't quite figure out what it is. I bet you could tell me, couldn't you?"

Mom stood quietly with her head down, but her lips were tight. She said nothing, but dad kept glaring at her. I was feeling almost dizzy.

Then it happened. There was another Angie there. Only it wasn't Anjie. Not at all. This Angie was me, me all the way, only better. This one was me and the Lord. He was right there.

"We don't have to have bacon at all," I said. "We can have tortilla chips, and Jason is going to make milk shakes. Then Shelley made some cherry Jell-O, and we have a cake. It doesn't go up high in the middle like I thought it would, but it's OK. I think I can figure out how to make coffee if you and mom want to sit down in the living room and visit a few minutes."

"It seems to me I better go," dad said, quietly. He looked at mom.

Again, the other Angie spoke. "At least stay until you have a cup of coffee, dad. We can sort of start over and try to do it more nicely." *Nicely* is a word I never use, but it seemed to get his attention.

Then I looked at mom. She was frozen, like she gets sometimes when she doesn't know what to do and she feels terrible. I was more surprised than anyone, but I just walked over to her and slipped my arm around her waist. "Mom let us make out the grocery list and buy whatever we wanted."

Suddenly it was so quiet in the kitchen that the old, wheezing electric clock could be heard all over the room. That clock has always done that, but we all just stood and listened to it. Then mom began to brush my hair behind my ear with an icy finger. She did it over and over, real slowly. Finally she said, "I'm sorry I was so awful about the bacon, Angie." She started to cry. "What have I done?" She pulled me real close to her. That got me started.

My dad stood there a minute watching us; then he walked over. Slowly he put one of his hands on each of our shoulders. I moved over closer to him, so that brought mom over, too. Then I put my arm around him, and he put his arm around me and mom.

"I'm sorry, too, Angie," he said. We were all kinda melted together, and we moved slightly to shift our weight. That's when I looked across the room and saw Jason, still sitting on the floor. His face was so tired and sad, and he was rubbing his shoulder where he had hit the cabinet.

Don't ask me why I never noticed this before, but it came to me like a bolt of lightning. I said to myself, *He's only a little boy.* I could not get over it. It was like I couldn't believe it was so obvious, and I had never seen it. *He's just a little boy,* I kept thinking. I wanted to grab my parents and show them how little Jason was.

Finally I said, "I just remembered that it takes quite a lot of time to get coffee water hot on this burner, so if you want to bat Jason a few grounders, I know you'll have time before we eat."

My dad looked at Jason. He let go of us and kind of clapped his hands together once. "Grounders, huh?" he said with a bright, false gaiety. "I better not bat any grounders to old Jason here or they're liable to whiz right past him into the street."

Jason pulled one of the leather strings on his mitt. "Uh-uh," he said with an effort.

"You don't think so?" Dad was beginning to sound like himself again. "What will you give me for every grounder that I get past you into the street?"

Jason grinned. "There won't be any."

"Well, but what if there are? Let's make a deal."

"OK." Jason's face lit up. "If you get one in the street, I'll rub your feet for one minute, and if I stop one, you have to tickle my back."

Dad considered it. "Let's say you get a point for every grounder you stop, and I get one for every one that gets away. The first one to get ten gets the foot rub."

"Or the back tickle," Jason said.

"Or the back tickle."

Shelley stood leaning against the bathroom door, sucking her thumb.

"Shelley, you can go and watch dad and Jason, or you can help set the table," I said. But Shelley said nothing. She stood watching for a minute while Jason and dad were waiting for her to decide. Then she ran to dad and threw her arms around his knee and hugged it as tight as she could. Her eyes were red and her cheeks were streaked, but her curls looked kinda bouncy and cheerful against his pant leg.

"Hey," he said softly. He leaned down and picked her up. "Did you know that your front door giggles when you try to shut it?" She snuggled up to his neck, and he carried her towards the door.

Jason followed, dragging his bat across the rug. "Hey, dad!" he said. "Let's say that you get two points for stopping a fly ball. Want to?"

Dad turned around. "Hey, Carolyn. You better come out here. I think our son is trying to hustle me from the sound of things."

Mom wiped her eyes on a dish towel.

"Go on, mom," I said. "I want to do the bacon all by myself and everything else is ready."

So she did. After a while, mom came back in and got me. We all played baseball until almost quarter to nine. Then we ate.

Dad and mom went and got dad's stuff the next day. The trial separation was over. We're still not the world's greatest, every minute, that's for sure. But I think the Lord has hopes for us.

Ready For More Great Reading From David C. Cook?

FOR AGES 9-14

Dear Angie, Your Family Is Getting A Divorce

Mom and Dad's marriage problems make junior-high growing pains even worse.

BY CAROL NELSON

Angie's world seems to fall apart when her parents announce a trial separation. How can this happen to a Christian family? How will they cope? Is it her fault?

Dear Angie, Your Family is Getting a Divorce #52464—$2.50

The Gitaway Box

An old man and a boy run away from home...and make some surprising discoveries

BY HILARY MILTON

Threatened with being sent to institutions, a boy and his grandfather set out on foot to find a new home...an experience that forces the boy "to grow up" and helps him claim his grandfather's deep faith in God for himself.

The Gitaway Box #52431—$2.95

The Secret Of The Spanish Treasure
Mystery and excitement at summer camp
BY JAN WASHBURN
14-year old Lark Ellison's first experience as a camp counselor includes
more than she'd expected...a puzzling relationship with a boy named
Stormy, and a mystery she helps him solve.
The Secret of the Spanish Treasure **#52456—$2.50**

The Blessing Deer
A teen-ager finds that she can't hide from racial prejudice
BY LOIS HENDERSON
A carved wooden deer from an Indian friend becomes the symbol of
teen-age Ellen's growing understanding of racial prejudice and how it
affects her friends, her family—even her church.
The Blessing Deer **#52449—$2.95**

CHOOSE HERE...CLIP THE COUPON...ENCLOSE WITH YOUR PAYMENT—AND WE'LL DO THE REST!
(OR VISIT YOUR FAVORITE CHRISTIAN BOOKSTORE)

David C. Cook Publishing Co.
Attn: Jenny Van Treese
850 North Grove Avenue
Elgin, IL 60120

Name_____

Address_____

City_____State_____Zip _____

Telephone Number _____/ _____
(We will telephone you if we have a question about your order)

BOOK TITLE	ORDER NO.	PRICE	QTY.	TOTAL

Enclose: *Enclose 75¢ per book shipping & handling.
☐ check   Illinois & California residents, add applicable sales tax.
☐ money order   Credit Card
☐ MasterCard   Account No. _____
☐ Visa   Signature of
               Authorized Buyer_____

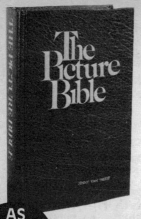

Order The Deluxe Picture Bible... And We'll Personalize It FREE!

ONLY $12.95
(plus $1.35 shipping and handling per book)

AS SEEN ON TV!

THE PERFECT FIRST BIBLE FOR CHILDREN

- alive with color—over 750 pages unfold the stories of the Bible *including* both the Old and the New Testaments
- its picture-strip look is fun and easy to read—a boon in helping children understand the Bible
- a wonderful gift to cherish and share
- guidelines for a lifetime
- we'll stamp the name of your choice in golden-look lettering right on the deluxe leather-look Red cover

Simply Clip The Coupon...Enclose Your Payment...and We'll Do The Rest!
(Or Visit Your Favorite Christian Bookstore!)

David C. Cook Publishing Co.
ATTN: Jenny Van Treese
850 North Grove Avenue
Elgin, IL 60120

Name _____

Address _____

City_____ State_____ Zip _____

Please send me_____copies of the Deluxe Picture Bible #52241 at $12.95 plus $1.35 shipping and handling.

Name To Be Inscribed

[ ]

Enclose:

☐ check

☐ money order

☐ MasterCard

☐ Visa

*If you are ordering more than one Bible, please enclose additional names, printed on a separate sheet of paper. Illinois & California residents please add appropriate sales tax.

Credit Card Account No. _____

Signature of Authorized Buyer _____

We'd Like To Introduce You To Exciting... Inspirational and Downright Fun Books (For The Entire Family) From David C. Cook!

Books for every age...hardbound encyclopedias and Bibles...compelling biographies of people in the limelight...briefcase size books of inspiration for the busy commuter...delightful books for children from 3 to 14...romance, mystery and suspense with a uniquely spiritual flavor for women...too many to list!

SIMPLY CLIP THE COUPON AND SEND IT TO THE ADDRESS BELOW...AND WE'LL SEND YOU A FREE CATALOG!

- -

**YES...
PLEASE SEND ME
A FREE CATALOG OF
DAVID C. COOK BOOKS!**

David C. Cook Publishing Co.
ATTN: Jenny Van Treese
850 North Grove Ave.
Elgin, IL 60120

Name_____

Address_____

City_____State_____Zip _____